'Open this window or I'll rear
sandwich!'

Robbie sat bolt upright on
because he really did not beli
seemed to be a crowd of small figures standing outside the
window and looking in over the heap of paperbacks. Their
shadows fell inwards over the sill. They varied in size, but
the very biggest was no bigger than a monkey. Some of
them wore coats with the collars turned up, and trilby hats,
puled down well over their faces.

'Are you going to let us in?' called one, 'or are we going to
blast this window all over town?'

Outside Robbie's window stood a tiny group of mini-
gangsters. As they huddled together peering in, they looked
exactly like the figures from the cover of *Gangsters 7* . . .

Glenn

Also available by Victoria Whitehead:

THE CHIMNEY WITCHES
CHIMNEY WITCH CHASE
CHIMNEY WITCH CHRISTMAS

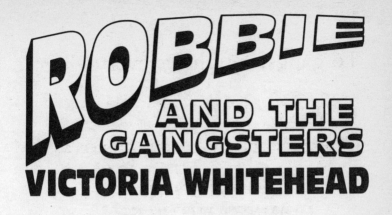

ROBBIE AND THE GANGSTERS

VICTORIA WHITEHEAD

Illustrated by Doffy Weir

YEARLING BOOKS

To gangster fighters everywhere

ROBBIE AND THE GANGSTERS

A YEARLING BOOK 0 440 86262 0

First published in Great Britain by Doubleday,
a division of Transworld Publishers Ltd

PRINTING HISTORY
Doubleday edition published 1991
Yearling edition published 1992

This book is set in 14/17pt Bembo by
Falcon Graphic Art Ltd

Yearling Books are published by Transworld Publishers Ltd,
61–63 Uxbridge Road, Ealing, London W5 5SA, in Australia by
Transworld Publishers (Australia) Pty Ltd, 15–23 Helles Avenue,
Moorebank, NSW 2170, and in New Zealand by Transworld Publishers
(NZ) Ltd, 3 William Pickering Drive, Albany, Auckland.

Printed and bound in Great Britain by
Cox & Wyman Ltd, Reading, Berks

Contents

1

Robbie's Day Off

It was a cold morning in late November and Robbie woke up, feeling horribly well as usual. He lay in bed wondering what it would be like to wake up feeling ill. The truth was that he did not want to go to school. Everyone in Robbie's block of flats had had at least one day off school with a cough or a cold or a sore throat by this time in the term, but Robbie never seemed to catch things like that. It wasn't fair.

It was Grandpa's eightieth birthday today and Robbie wanted to take him some books he had bought him as a present. Grandpa always said how much he enjoyed a 'blinking good read'. Robbie could buy old paperback books very cheap from Wusster's second-hand stall in the market. If he stayed off school, he knew that Grandpa would be pleased to see him. If he stayed off school, he knew he wouldn't have to see those kids he didn't like in his class – kids like the ones in Will Smith's gang. The gang who kept calling him Scraggs and Skinny and Stupid and other wallyish names like that. The gang he had told he had a black belt in karate and that he was junior champion of the world!

He kicked the covers off his bed and lay still for a bit. Then he climbed out of bed and stood, dressed only in boxer shorts and a T-shirt, next to his open window. That made him shiver. His teeth began to chatter. If he stood there long enough, he thought, with a bit of luck he might manage to catch a cold. He flexed his biceps muscles, first on one arm and then on the other. He could make them feel quite hard when he tensed his arm and when he clenched his fist they bulged like hamburger rolls. He might be skinny, but he was strong.

Standing shivering in the cold bedroom air was a stupid thing to do. He knew that. It was almost as stupid as telling someone you had a black belt in karate when you didn't. Why had he told Will Smith's gang that? He should have told them he was junior skateboarding champion of the whole world instead. He wasn't brilliant at skateboarding but he was a darned

sight better at it than he was at karate. The truth was that he couldn't do karate at all.

Robbie pulled on some clothes – old jeans and a sweater – and went out of the front door of the flat, being careful not to make a noise. He ran down the stairs to the ground floor of the block, scooping up his skateboard from under the stairs as he ran out into the street. It was misty outside. The houses looked like toys gift-wrapped in cellophane. The mist made Robbie shiver even harder than before.

He jumped on his skateboard and sped off along the pavement. He came off the skateboard only twice in twenty metres. He thought he was improving. He rattled on down the road past McReady's Hamburger Bar where he could smell the McReady breakfast cooking. He was soon in the square where the market would be set up later. Some of the rubbish left from yesterday's market still lay there, moving slightly on the tarmac. He jumped off his skateboard to cross the road between the market square and the park. Just one car went by. He waited, then crossed, and sailed smoothly through the park gates to the swings. He was pleased with himself. He thought he was skateboarding brilliantly.

But when Robbie arrived at the swings he had a very nasty shock. He saw Will Smith there. He wondered what Will was doing up at that time of the morning, zooming round and round on the roundabout at a hundred revs per minute. Robbie was not just surprised to see Will, he was really fed up as well. He was out here to try and catch a cold before breakfast and Will Smith was the last person he wanted to see.

He had had to tell Will and the whole gang that he had a black belt in karate because it was the only way to impress them and make them shut up. All he had wanted was to be left alone. But now Will Smith had fixed up a match between Robbie and some other boy who really *was* brilliant at karate. The other boy's dad owned a gym, and was a karate expert. That other boy had been learning karate since he was three. The karate match was all fixed up for dinner break in school that day.

Robbie did not have a hope of winning. Apart from reading one book about it once he didn't know anything about karate at all. He didn't know how to get out of the fix he was in. All he knew just at the moment was that he had to find a way to stay off school.

'Hey, Scraggs!' called Will Smith, when he

saw Robbie approaching. 'In training for the karate match, are you? Twelve-thirty on the school field today? You haven't forgotten, have you?'

'Don't know, not sure, really,' called Robbie, as he skateboarded swiftly past Will, making sure he was going much too fast to stop. 'I might not be feeling well today. I might be going to be ill later. I might have to stay off school!'

By the time he had finished speaking he was way past Will. He did a fancy turn on the skateboard by dipping its back until it scraped along the ground, shooting up dust, and tipping its front towards the trees at an angle of forty-five degrees. Off Robbie scooted, back towards the gate of the park. He was behind a cluster of trees before he fell off.

'Phew,' he thought, 'thank goodness for that.'

He stayed off the skateboard to dart across the road, then climbed on it again to weave amongst the various market stalls that had now appeared in the square.

2

The F.F.F.M.M.M.

Some of the stall-holders in the market were just setting up. Robbie slipped between the stall where the T-shirts would be later, and the shell-fish stall, which had nothing on it yet, although the fishy smell still lingered. He stopped at the place where the second-hand books would be sold. This was where he had bought the karate book and some others for Grandpa's eightieth birthday. There were a few books out on display on the stall already, but most of them were still in boxes in the back of an old blue van with DASH'S BOOKS written on the side.

Wusster Dash, who ran this second-hand book stall, sold really special books. A lot of them were very old and tattered, but they somehow felt alive. That was why Robbie liked to browse around the stall and, when he had some money to spend (which was not often), to spend it there. Robbie sometimes thought that the alive feeling might have something to do with the weird experiments Wusster occasionally did on the paperback books people gave him to sell. Wusster Dash spent all his spare time inventing strange machines and doing mad experiments on books.

Little wonder then that he was known in Stack Green as the local weirdo. He had a stubbly beard and was always dressed the same, wearing an ancient black quilted anorak, a battered maroon hat and a very long, loosely knitted scarf wrapped several times around his neck, no matter how warm the weather. The machines Wusster invented were weird, machines which looked as though they had been stuck together in a moment and would never be of any use to anyone. He often brought them to his stall so that he could tinker with them while he was selling books. What was not generally known in Stack Green was that Wusster had a secret – a secret formula passed down to him through many generations of inventors. The truth was that he was on the brink of an absolutely amazing and truly mind-boggling discovery.

Robbie sometimes talked to Wusster about

his machines, because he often skateboarded around the market and usually ended up looking through the second-hand books. He liked looking through the sort of books that Grandpa liked – books with thrilling adventures, brave detectives and lurid covers. 'They don't write books like those any more,' Grandpa used to say. When Robbie had found a book about karate on the stall, he had read it from cover to cover. He knew really, though, that if he was to get out of the fix he now found himself in, he needed more help than just a book could give him.

There was a larger-than-average machine standing on the end of Wusster's stall today. It was an iron box with wires tangled around it like spaghetti and it was about the size of a dog-kennel. It had tubes for sucking things in and holes for bilging things out. There was something that looked like a clock clamped to the top and several aerials clustered at one end. Switches were clicking, wheels were whirring and lights were flashing and Robbie was curious to know what was going on.

He stepped off his skateboard, holding it still with one foot, and peered at the strangely concocted machine.

'What's this one for, Wusster?' he asked.

Wusster was on his hands and knees under the machine with his head hidden inside. He pulled his head out and smiled.

'Oh, good morning, Robbie,' he said. 'Ah, now that's the sixty-four-thousand dollar question.'

He spoke with a middle European accent and waved his hands around as he talked.

'This machine, Robbie,' he went on, climbing to his feet and wiping his hands on his scarf, 'is the culmination of all my years of experiments. This is the Mark 72 F.F.F.M.M.M. My Fantastic Fact to Fiction Magic Moderating Module – F.F.M. for short. This, Robbie, is the *big* one.'

He tapped the side of the machine affectionately with his screwdriver.

'Doesn't look that big to me,' Robbie said, frowning and wondering what all Wusster's excitement could be about.

Wusster looked at Robbie for a moment, then threw his head back and laughed like a donkey braying. He had three gold teeth.

'This is the machine,' said Wusster, moving closer to Robbie, 'that will eventually be able to mix fact with fiction, reality with fantasy – things that happen in books with things that happen in real life. You see what I mean now Robbie? The *big* one.'

Robbie was still perplexed. Everyone had always told him that Wusster had a screw loose. Robbie had always said he wasn't so sure. But this did seem to be an exceptionally screwy idea.

'You put books in that machine . . .?' Robbie began.

'Yes,' said Wusster. 'Here.' And he indicated a square dish in which a book could be placed and slid into the machine. 'I have experimented with many books already,' Wusster went on, 'including the ones you bought for your grandpa.'

'. . . and one day, you will be able to make people in books come *alive*?' asked Robbie, amazed.

'Not yet, you understand,' Wusster said, holding up a cautionary hand. 'Not today, maybe, or even tomorrow. But next week perhaps. Soon the machine will be able to do that . . . *soon*.'

All in a moment, like lightning striking a conductor, Robbie had a brilliant idea.

'That karate book I bought from you a few weeks ago, you remember?' he said.

Wusster nodded.

'Can you bring that karate teacher alive to give me lessons?' he asked eagerly. 'You see,' he jiggled his skateboard around with his foot, 'you see, I'm in trouble with this gang in school and if I could do karate everything would be all right.'

Wusster thought about that for a moment, nodded his head, then shook it again. Then he laughed loudly, a donkey laugh which made people arriving in the market square stop and look. Wusster clamped a heavy hand on Robbie's shoulder.

'Not yet, Robbie,' he said. 'But one day, YES!'

Robbie wondered how long he could manage to stay off school. Until Wusster managed to get his machine to work perhaps? How soon was soon? If Wusster's F.F.M. could really be made to work one day that would be completely, blinking, brilliant!

Robbie looked at the time on the clock fixed to the top of the F.F.M. It was nearly eight o'clock. His mother would be up by now.

'I'd better go,' he said. 'Got to get back home. Mum will be wondering where I am.'

'Goodbye, Robbie. Give my regards to your grandpa when you see him,' muttered Wusster distractedly. 'Wish him a happy birthday from me.' He put his head back inside the F.F.M. and a bright green light started flashing. A loud buzzing began, as if there was a bee trapped in a bottle somewhere.

3

The Excuses Racket Begins

Robbie skateboarded home and pranced up the three steps that led to the main front door. He left his skateboard beneath the stairs and jogged energetically up to flat number seven, where he lived with his mum on the second floor. He let himself into the flat quietly, not slamming the door and shouting as he usually did, but creeping straight to his room. He felt warm now and a bit sweaty. He threw off his clothes and scrambled into his pyjamas, emerging only seconds later with a mournful look on his face. He hoped he might have caught a cold in the chilly mist that morning, but knew it was a long shot. Even if he had caught a cold it would not show itself for a while. Until then he would have to pretend.

He staggered into the kitchen, where Mum

was making breakfast, and slumped down at the table as if he was about to breathe his last.

He looked at his bacon sandwich and groaned quietly. After several minutes, it became clear that his mother, who was looking in a mirror and putting on a very long pair of earrings, was not going to notice without help. He groaned again and said in a trembling voice, 'I don't feel well this morning.'

'Get on with you,' said Mum briskly as she used two hands to flatten down her grey fitted skirt. 'Finish your breakfast and off you go to school.'

Robbie coughed weakly and said, 'I think I've got a cold.'

'Just a sniffle, I expect,' said Mum.

'. . . and I feel hot,' Robbie added. 'I may have a temperature as well.'

'Oh dear,' said Mum, who was wanting to get off to the shop where she worked every morning. 'Well, just sit down in the armchair for a moment, love, will you, while I fetch the thermometer.'

She whipped the bacon sandwich away from under his nose and threw it in the bin. Robbie put his hand over his mug of tea when Mum tried to take it away, to show that he thought he might just manage to drink it if she left it a while.

Mum was much too busy organizing the contents of her handbag and looking for her front-door keys, to stand over Robbie while the thermometer was in his mouth. That meant that she did not see him take it out for a moment and gulp some warm tea from the mug. He washed the tea over his tongue, swallowed it quickly and replaced the thermometer. Exactly three minutes later, Mum took the thermometer out of Robbie's mouth.

She did not tell him what the reading on the thermometer was, but he could see that it was high by the way her brow furrowed and her face paled as she looked at it.

'Oh well, Robbie love,' she said with a loud sigh of resignation as she shook the thermometer sharply and put it away. 'That's that, I suppose. No school for you with a fever so high. It looks as if we're both going to have to stay at home this morning.'

She took off her earrings and slammed them down on the dresser, then she kissed Robbie's forehead.

'You go back to bed now and I'll ring the shop,' she said.

Robbie was so triumphant that he almost forgot to look miserable as he left the room. When he reached his bedroom, he leapt, panther-like, into bed and realized with a little start of surprise that he had actually made it. He'd missed the karate match and had won himself a day off school into the bargain. He could watch television all morning and go and see Grandpa and give him the books for his birthday that afternoon. Black Belt Karate Champ he might not be, but Excuses Champ he certainly was!

Robbie, still in his pyjamas, was lying flat on his bedspread. He crossed his legs, stretched them and felt the muscles on them. Then he put both hands behind his head. He made a few drum noises with his tongue against the top of his mouth, then got up and walked across to his desk by the window to flick through Grandpa's birthday books. They had wonderful titles like *Gangsters 7, The Oriental Gems* and *The Karate Champ*. Robbie began to feel the way he often did, looking through books from Wusster's stall. Something about those paperbacks felt unusually exciting and alive.

He picked up *Gangsters 7*, which had a picture of a group of desperate-looking villains on the

front. He took a flying leap across the room on to his bed. Lying on his side, he began to leaf through the book. It was a book for grown-ups. Too old for him, really. Not the sort of thing he would generally read. Too many words. But passages out of it were brilliant, and he liked the way it felt.

Robbie never knew what made him glance across the room just then. Perhaps it was a noise – a shuffling noise – or the muffled murmur of voices. He blinked his eyes hard then blinked them again, because he thought he saw something strange move across the windowpane. A grey shadow was blowing like a silk scarf across the sill. As he lay watching, the shadow softly shifted across the books piled there. Robbie's mouth fell open . . .

4

Gangsters 7

'Hey, kid, you in there, open up!' demanded a voice like an electric saw. 'Open this window or I'll rearrange it with a ton of knuckle sandwich!'

Robbie sat bolt upright on the bed. He rubbed his eyes because he really did not believe what he could see. There seemed to be a crowd of small figures standing outside the window and looking in over the heap of paperbacks. Their shadows fell inwards over the sill. They varied in size, but the very biggest was no bigger than a monkey. Some of them wore coats with the collars turned up, and trilby hats, pulled down well over their faces.

'Are you going to let us in?' called one, 'or are we going to blast this window all over town?'

Outside Robbie's window stood a tiny group

of mini-gangsters. As they huddled together peering in, they looked exactly like the figures from the cover of *Gangsters* 7.

Robbie glanced down at the open book he had slammed down beside him on the bed, bashed his forehead with the back of his hand and seriously wondered whether he was going screwy like Wusster Dash. But when he looked again, the figures were still outside.

Fired by great waves of curiosity, he bounded out of bed to open the window. Three of the little men skipped inside. Four more waited on the sill outside, looking outwards, keeping guard. Of the three who came inside, one was clearly a leader. He was much smaller than the others but his coat had a fur collar and he had a diamond ring on one of his chubby fingers. He jumped down on to Robbie's desk, took off his coat and motioned to one of the others to take the coat and to bring him a box to sit on. A bald and muscly member of the group did that. The boss kept his trilby hat on and so did the third man. They all had mean eyes and scarred cheeks and were obviously gangsters – crooks of the most desperate and villainous kind. Robbie stared at them, quite unable to believe his eyes.

'Is this the boy who wants a day off school,

Mr Boscoff?' said the man with the bulging muscles and a nose squashed flat like a boxer's.

His voice was like the bottom of a river.

'Yes, Fist, I believe it is,' said Mr Boscoff, in a thin voice like string.

This was the man who was clearly the boss.

'Can I show him the gear, then?' said the third man, who had a bright tie and a tiny black moustache and was bursting with nervous energy.

Without waiting for an answer, he dropped a case on the desk and flipped it open expertly.

'Yes, Smarto, the gear, all in good time,' said Mr Boscoff, slowly looking Robbie up and down. 'But first, we have something most important to ask him.'

'Right, Boss,' said Fist, nodding his head in agreement.

'Right, Boss,' said Smarto, cheerfully. 'Ask him if he's seen the girl.'

'Girl?' echoed Robbie, mystified.

'There's a girl,' said Boscoff. 'An oriental girl, a jewel thief. Are you hiding her here?'

'A jewel thief? Of course not!' said Robbie, all innocence, but his eye wandered to the pile of books that had been knocked skew-wiff when the gangsters had come in through the window. On the cover of *The Oriental Gems*, he could clearly see a picture of a girl. She was crouching behind something and seemed to be very frightened. There were jewels strewn all around her feet. Could she be the girl they were talking about? Surely not. It was just a story. He shook his head again.

'No?' said Fist.

'No,' said Robbie.

'He says "no", Mr Boscoff,' said Fist.

'Can we get on with showing him the stuff then, Mr Boscoff?' said Smarto, impatiently.

Mr Boscoff took a mint humbug out of his pocket, unwrapped it and put it in his mouth before he spoke.

'All right, Smarto,' he said. 'Go ahead. Show the boy the gear. Shoot!'

Robbie wondered for a moment what Boscoff wanted Smarto to shoot. But it turned out to be a line. Smarto talked like an expert salesman. His line was very fast and very smooth.

'You want a day off school?' he said to Robbie, with an amiable smile, 'so how are you off for excuses?'

'Excuses?' said Robbie, bemused. 'Excuses? Oh, I've got plenty already.'

'Well,' Smarto went on, 'you see, young

Robbie – may I call you Robbie?'

Robbie nodded.

'Well, you see, young Robbie,' Smarto continued, 'we've got such a range of excuses here that if you want to do business with Mr Boscoff, we can guarantee you as many days off school as you want, for the rest of your life!'

Well, that sounded all right for a start.

'How?' asked Robbie, all ears.

'Well,' continued Smarto, 'Mr Boscoff and us boys here are currently running a little excuses racket.'

'Racket?' said Robbie.

Excuses were one thing, but the only 'racket' he knew anything about was the kind you use to play tennis.

'Yes,' said Smarto. 'It's like this, you see. If you make an excuse, in school, what do you need to back it up?'

Boscoff snapped his fingers at Fist for a reply.

'Evidence,' said Fist, looking pleased with himself.

'And what have we got here in the case?' Smarto went on.

'*Evidence!*' cried Fist, looking even more delighted. '*Excuses* evidence!'

'Like what?' Robbie asked, intrigued.

'Bogus dentist appointment cards, bruised thumbs, fake sneezes, thermometers stuck at thirty-nine degrees celsius,' Smarto began. 'You name it, we've got it.'

As Smarto went through the list, Fist produced wodges of papers and boxes and packets out of his case, held them up in the air for inspection and then slammed them down on to the desk. Mr Boscoff sat back on his box, sucking his humbug and looking like a cat which has just drunk twenty cartons of cream.

'Evidence, you see,' continued Smarto. 'Evidence to support any excuse any kid might ever dream up. We can supply it by the suitcase-full . . . although, naturally, it doesn't come cheap!'

Mr Boscoff smiled good-naturedly, stood up and walked over to Robbie.

'So what do you say, Robbie, boy?' he asked pleasantly. 'Would you like to buy some excuses from Mr Boscoff? Mr Boscoff's racket does very well in Paperbackstack. Would you like to help set it up here in Stack Green?'

Robbie had to give this offer some very careful thought. The main problem being that he didn't have any money. He had spent his last penny on paperbacks for Grandpa. He was stony broke. He thought he had better come clean and tell the gangsters straight.

He smiled, as all the little men were smiling at him now, and sat down on his bed, shaking his head apologetically.

'No,' he said, 'I'm afraid not. I can't afford to buy any excuses.'

The smiles faded suddenly from all the gangsters' faces and Fist stepped forward grimly.

'People don't, in general, say "no" to Mr Boscoff,' he pointed out. His hands were clenched like two cauliflowers.

'Well.' said Boscoff, making a circular motion with his bejewelled hand to beckon Robbie closer. 'In that case, perhaps you would like to help us by selling our excuses to your friends?'

'You want me to help you *sell* things?' cried Robbie, more loudly than he had intended.

'Yes,' said Boscoff, mildly. 'We have very good commission terms.'

Robbie wondered for a moment if he could. The only stuff he'd ever been asked to sell before had been raffle tickets for the Scouts and he had lost all those before he'd had time to sell them. His mum had been a bit upset about missing the chance of winning a holiday for two in Amsterdam. In fact, she had got quite cross.

When Robbie thought about how cross it would make his mother if he got caught up in a gangster racket like this one, he decided quite quickly that his answer to the gangsters still had to be no. They were pretty small gangsters. He wasn't going to be bullied into anything by them.

He shook his head and worked out a hurried excuse.

'I don't think I can help you sell excuses,' he said. 'I'm almost always ill and I almost never go out. I don't often see other children to sell things to.'

It wasn't much of an excuse really, but it was all he could dream up at a moment's notice.

'Well, you know, kid, I like you,' said Mr Boscoff as he got up from his box, 'and I think that when you've given the matter some further consideration, you might like to change your mind.'

He stood up, reached forward and pressed a small calling card into Robbie's hand and then waited regally while Fist hung his coat around his shoulders.

'You think it over, Robbie boy,' he said at last. 'And, if you do have a change of heart, come along to Slim Jim's Gym and Health Club, in Paperbackstack. One of the gang will get in touch with you there.'

Robbie looked briefly at the calling card in his hand. On one side he read *Compliments of the*

Boscoff Boys, and on the other side was printed *Slim Jim's Gym and Health Club*. Underneath that was an address.

'Do they do karate at this gym club?' Robbie asked the gangster boss.

'They certainly do, Robbie boy,' said Boscoff. 'Karate, they certainly do.'

That's absolutely blinking brilliant, Robbie thought.

Smarto gathered up all the things that he had taken out of his case, and the three visitors climbed out on to the windowsill, where the other four had been waiting. All seven gangsters dropped from view as mysteriously as they had appeared. Robbie dashed to the window and looked out but all he could see were some autumn leaves floating down to the street below.

Robbie looked again at the calling card the gangsters had left with him. *Compliments of the Boscoff Boys*. He turned it over. *Slim Jim's Gym and Health Club*. And then he noticed there was something else written on the card. Something pencilled in, scrawled, written roughly by someone in a hurry.

3 Monsters

7 Dreams

9 Pops

That's all

Robbie furrowed his brow and scratched his head. He did not have the slightest idea what that meant. But he did not even have time to wonder too hard at that moment. He slipped the card between the pages of *Gangsters* 7, which had been left lying on his bed. As he did so, he noticed something extraordinary. The picture on the cover of the book had changed! The background was still there but there were seven white spaces, where previously the gangsters had been shown.

Robbie snatched it up in amazement. He was completely flabbergasted. Surely these small characters coming alive out of a book must have had something to do with Wusster's crazy F.F.M. machine. But Wusster had said his machine wasn't working yet. Robbie thought that he ought to get the books back to Wusster right away and tell him what had happened. He decided somewhat reluctantly that maybe excuses were not such a good way of wangling time off school after all. Gangsters were *bad*, weren't they? Of course they were. And he had to admit to himself that fibbing to stay off school was kind of bad as well. Poor Mum had had to stay off work to be at home with him that morning. He realized now that he really had not been fair.

Robbie jumped to his feet and got dressed again in jeans with tears at the knees and a sweatshirt with a skateboard motif.

'I think I'll go and tell Mum I feel better right now,' he resolved. 'I'm not too keen on this excuses racket after all.' And with that, he marched purposefully back to the living-room, where Mum had just finished speaking on the phone.

5

The Further Adventures of Spiff

'Robbie, you're dressed,' Mum said in surprise when she saw him.

'Yes, I feel better,' said Robbie coyly.

'What!' exclaimed Mum so loudly that Robbie lost his nerve.

'Better,' he said. 'Not good, though. I don't think you should stay off work just for me.'

Mum smiled.

'It can't be helped,' she said warmly. 'I'll have to ring the shop and tell them I can't work today. But, I'll tell you what, if you *are* feeling a little better, I'll take you to the doctor's surgery. That'll save him coming here.'

Robbie had to agree.

It was later in the morning when Robbie and his mum set off on the short walk that took them along the street, through the market and across the park to the doctor's surgery. The mist of the morning had cleared to unveil a bright and bustling day. After an endless wait in a room full of people coughing and blowing their noses, Robbie finally got to see Dr Ericson, who started by taking his temperature and said it was fine. Mum looked surprised and then relieved. Next the doctor looked down Robbie's throat, then he listened to his lungs, then checked his ears and said they were all absolutely A-one. He suggested that Robbie's mother might buy him some pastilles for his throat and told him to keep warm for the rest of the day. By tomorrow he thought he should be perfectly well.

As Robbie and his mum sauntered back across the park, Robbie told her that he didn't mind waiting by the swings, while she went over the road to a nearby chemist for some throat pastilles. He thought he would see if he could zoom round and round on the roundabout as fast as Will Smith had done that morning.

He settled himself on the roundabout and pushed hard with one foot. Round he sped like a picture on a spinning top. But when he came round for the fourth or the fifth time, his gaze was attracted by a pile of dead leaves at the edge of the playground. He thought he saw something moving behind it.

'A squirrel,' he thought, 'or a small dog.'

He came round again. This time he was convinced that there was something odder than that. After going round once more, he jumped off the roundabout to investigate. As he approached the pile there was a scuffling noise as whatever it was stepped out from behind the trunk of a tree. Robbie peered down, blinked and looked again.

A miniature boy was standing there. A boy of about Robbie's age, maybe a year or two older, but a quarter the size. Maybe the size of a monkey. The boy was dressed very oddly indeed. He was in a tweedy suit, with trousers that finished at the knees. The bottom halves of his legs were covered with long black woollen socks. He had bubbly, curly, sandy-coloured hair and wire-rimmed spectacles perched precariously on his nose. When he smiled confidently up at Robbie, who was a giant in comparison, he displayed two of the largest front teeth that Robbie had ever seen.

'What ho, old chap,' he said.

'What ho?' said Robbie. 'Whatever do you mean?'

'Well, one thing's for sure. I don't want to be a bother to you,' was the reply. 'I was just hoping that you might be able to spare a few minutes to assist me with some enquiries,' and he stepped boldly from behind the tree and fell straight down a rabbit hole.

'Enquiries?' exclaimed Robbie, helping the boy out of the hole and handing him his glasses, which had fallen into a patch of dandelions. 'What do you mean, "enquiries"?' he said.

'Well, old fellow, pin back your ears,' said the boy, 'and I will explain.' He twitched his nose and grinned toothily.

'I come from a book called *Spiff Solves Another Riddle*,' he began. 'Carruthers is the name – Spiff Carruthers, intrepid boy detective. How do you do?' He held his hand out to shake Robbie's.

'How do you do?' said Robbie, feeling weird, and they shook hands.

'Perhaps you would care to glance at this,' Spiff went on. He took a rolled-up newspaper from inside his jacket and waved it in front of Robbie. 'Would you oblige me by looking briefly at that article on the front?' Spiff said.

Robbie took the paper from him and looked at the front page. The paper was called the

Paperbackstack Chronicle and the leading headline ran like this:

PAPERBACKSTACK EXCUSES RACKET SPREADS

The article was printed so small that Robbie had trouble reading it, even with his eyes screwed up. The boy cheerfully produced a large magnifying glass from inside his jacket and handed it to Robbie. The glass was tiny for Robbie, enormous for the boy. Using that, Robbie read further.

> *Reports were today confirmed that the world-famous gangland leader, Alberto Boscoff, has been looking for agents in Stack Green to help spread his excuses racket. 'We can cause such chaos with children staying off school and adults staying off work,' said a spokesman for the gangsters, 'that soon many organizations will have to close. That's very good for us gangsters because then we can take those organizations over.'*

'Schools to close?' said Robbie, thinking. 'That's absolutely blinking brilliant!'

'Yes, real rotten apples, these hoodlums,' said the boy, shaking his head in concern.

'Poor show, isn't it? Paperbackstack has appalling troubles that could spread here too.' His face brightened then as he looked straight up at Robbie. 'It is my fervent hope, however, that you will be able to give me the necessary information to foil the gangsters' plot.'

'Help you foil the gangsters' plot?' Robbie echoed, scratching his head. 'Do you come from Paperbackstack?' he asked, as he struggled to make sense of what he was hearing.

'No, I come from Hardback,' said the boy. 'I'd have thought that was plainly obvious to anybody. *Spiff Solves Another Riddle*. That's the name of my book. I told you. The series is *Further Adventures of Spiff*.'

Robbie had never heard of the book. He supposed that it must be another one from Wusster's stall. Perhaps it had gone through the F.F.M. machine as well. He shrugged. Nothing was plainly obvious to him any more.

'So what information can you give me?' Spiff asked Robbie, taking a notepad and a chewed-up stub of pencil out of his trouser pocket with the air of one who means business. He looked at Robbie searchingly. Robbie was too perplexed to answer.

'I believe the Boscoff boys paid you a visit

earlier this morning . . . at eight-fifteen to be precise,' Spiff observed, with a grin that revealed a lot more big teeth behind the ones at the front.

Robbie was astonished. How could Spiff possibly have known that that had happened and the exact time it had happened as well? He swallowed hard and went pink and hot. He wondered if Spiff knew that he had actually considered *helping* the gangsters. He blinking well hoped he didn't.

'Yes, I saw them,' he admitted hesitantly. 'They came to my flat.'

'I'm all ears, old fellow,' Spiff said keenly. 'Tell me what you know.'

'Oh, I don't *know* anything,' Robbie answered. 'They didn't tell me anything at all.'

'Visited you, stayed in your room for twenty minutes and didn't tell you anything at all?' said Spiff doubtfully. 'Come now, I find that hard to believe.'

'They didn't tell me anything but they gave me something,' Robbie said cautiously.

Spiff's eyes lit up with interest. Robbie went on.

'They gave me a gangster calling card with

things written on it, names, addresses, a list of words . . .'

'Go on, go on,' urged Spiff eagerly.

'Well, just one name and only one address, actually,' Robbie told him. He was having to wrack his brains to remember exactly what was written on the card.

'Yes, yes,' Spiff urged.

'The address was somewhere in Paperback-stack,' Robbie said thoughtfully. 'It wasn't the gangsters' headquarters or anything like that, but it was somewhere I could get in touch with them if I decided that I . . . er . . . wanted to.'

'Oh I say, that's just splendiferously super!' Spiff exclaimed, regarding Robbie intently. 'The address now. Go ahead. Tell me what it is.'

Spiff lifted his hand to push his glasses up his nose, but instead he knocked them off. While he was picking them up and carefully fixing each wire hook around each ear, Robbie took the opportunity to look up and check whether his mother had arrived back at the park gate to meet him. She had. She was standing there now, with her shopping at her feet, waving two hands above her head like two flags.

'Well?' Spiff asked, when he had finished with his spectacles, sucked his pencil lead and was ready to write again.

Robbie thought hard. 'I don't remember the address,' he admitted, 'but the name of the place was Skinny Jack's . . . no, Thin Bill's . . . no, Slim . . . Slim Jim's. Yes, now I remember. It was Slim Jim's Gym and Health Club!'

'Slim Jim's Gym and Health Club,' Spiff repeated the words slowly as he wrote them down.

'And the address?' he asked, looking up expectantly.

'Robbie! Robbie!' Robbie's mum was shouting very loudly now.

Robbie glanced first at his mum and then at Spiff.

'I'll have to go,' he said. 'The address is on the gangsters' calling card. It's in my room at home.'

'Yoohoo, Robbie!' Mum called. She sounded like a yodeller.

'Just a moment. Half a tick . . .' Spiff said. Without further ado, he scribbled a number on the top sheet of his pad and, tearing the page off, he handed it to Robbie. 'Go home with your mater now,' he instructed. 'When you find the address of Slim Jim's Gym and Health Club, telephone me. My number's on that sheet of paper. Remember, this information could be vital . . .'

Robbie put the number into the pocket of his jeans.

'Yes, I'll phone,' he promised, but he wasn't sure he would.

Spiff meanwhile replaced the newspaper, the magnifying glass, the notepad and the stub of pencil in various pockets in his clothing. He tossed his sandy curls and twitched the glasses on his nose. 'Till later then,' he said. 'Don't forget to phone.'

'I won't,' Robbie said, but at that moment, just as Spiff waved up at him and turned to leave, the strangeness of the situation struck him even more forcibly than it had before. He furrowed his brow and shook his head and slapped his cheek to see if he was dreaming.

'Blinking weird,' he muttered to himself. He turned and raced off, kicking up such a flurry of leaves that the boy detective was more or less buried. His muffled cries were soon lost in the roar of traffic beyond the railings and Robbie sprinted across the park to where his mother was waiting for him.

'Are you sure there's nothing wrong with your ears?' she shouted at him when he arrived. 'Whatever were you up to anyway?'

'I was talking to a chum, Mater,' said Robbie, grinning, and his mother looked at him oddly.

'Well, let's get home now,' Mum said after a second or two, during which they looked at each other without speaking and she felt his forehead with her hand to see how hot it was. 'It's chilly here,' she said. 'You shouldn't be out. I still don't think you're looking very well.'

6

The Market

When they arrived back at the block of flats it was late in the morning. Robbie glanced at his skateboard as he and Mum came inside the front door. It was standing by the stairway.

'Come on now, love,' Mum said as she started upstairs. 'Let's get into the warm. We don't want to make your cold worse, do we?' She reached the first-floor landing. 'I'm just going to phone Grandpa, to tell him you're ill and you won't be able to take the books round for him today. It's a shame. He'll be sorry, and on his eightieth birthday, too . . .'

She climbed up the next flight of stairs and opened the front door. She hadn't realized that Robbie was still standing at the bottom of the staircase, and he now had his skateboard in his hand.

'I've got a wobbly wheel on my skateboard,

Mum,' Robbie called upstairs. 'It needs check-ing out. Do you think I could muck about with it for a while? A bit longer outside won't make much difference, will it?'

He waited for an angry reaction from his mum but she clearly had her mind on her phone call and did not answer, so Robbie slid the skateboard to the doorway with a great rattle of wheels on the concrete floor. Then, he tipped it down the steps with his foot, climbed aboard and made off briskly and noisily along the path that ran out through the gate and on to the pavement.

He headed straight for the market. All the stalls were set up now and business was in full swing. He made a wide circle around the shell-fish, to avoid the smell, rattled by the T-shirts and then thundered on quickly to the second-hand books. He could see Wusster Dash talking to a customer.

Robbie jumped off his skateboard, stamped on the back and flicked it up, intending to catch it in his hand. He just missed, so he tried it again and missed again. He picked it up and leant it against one leg of the stall as Wusster's customer moved off.

'What's the matter, Robbie?' said Wusster

when he saw Robbie's face – flushed with excitement.

'Those books I bought for Grandpa,' Robbie gasped.

'The paperback crime thrillers? He liked them, yes?' Wusster enquired.

'He hasn't seen them yet,' Robbie began, 'but you know your F.F.M.?'

'Ah yes,' said Wusster, patting the machine as if it were a dog. 'Soon . . .'

'Well,' Robbie cut in excitedly. 'I think it may already be working.'

'What do you mean?' Wusster asked, his brow furrowed and his eyes questioning.

'I've met some gangsters,' Robbie told him, 'small gangsters. They say they come from a place called Paperbackstack, and I think that's in one of Grandpa's books!'

Wusster stared open-mouthed at Robbie. 'The machine is working?' he exclaimed. 'My F.F.M. is already working?'

The look on the bookseller's face was so incredulous that Robbie began to doubt his own story.

'Yes, and there's a boy detective too – I think – out of another book – I think – a hardback – I think – and he's chasing the gangsters – a least he says he is – and that's what seems to be happening – but I don't know if I can believe it – but I can – I think.'

Robbie wondered if he might be talking screwy nonsense, but Wusster had no doubts.

'Gangsters? Small gangsters? Walking about in Stack Green and talking to you?' he cried.

'Yes,' Robbie said with confidence. 'I think,' he added quietly.

Wusster grabbed Robbie by the arm.

'That boy detective – his name is Spiff?' he enquired, squeezing Robbie's arm so hard it hurt.

'That hardback book – it's called *Spiff Solves Another Riddle*!' Wusster continued, eyes wide with excitement. 'Robbie, tell me, is that right?' he urged. 'This is really of the utmost importance.'

'That's right!' said Robbie, nodding hard but feeling uncertain all the same.

Wusster let go of Robbie's arm and darted away for a moment. He grabbed a shabby old green hardback book from a pile on the other end of his stall and returned immediately. He held the book up square in front of Robbie's eyes.

'What do you see?' he asked.

What Robbie could see there, apart from a scorch mark on the cover, was a white shape. No picture, but the shape of a boy in a suit with knee-length trousers. Robbie could tell from the shape of the figure that the boy wore glasses and had bubbly hair. Robbie recognized him right away.

'The boy detective, the one I met!' he cried.

'That's right!' said Wusster, barely able to contain his jubilation. 'I put this hardback through the F.F.M. only this morning. And you are telling me that this character has come to life!'

Wusster shook his head, scratched his stubble, put the book down on the stall again and took Robbie by both shoulders.

'Fetch me your grandfather's paperback books as soon as you can,' he urged. 'We have to keep this experiment under control or we could let gangsters and other villains loose all over the place. There is still a great deal of work to be done on the F.F.M.'

Robbie nodded, and Wusster swung round to shout out to the crowds of milling shoppers bustling around the market. 'My machine,' he announced in a voice that made everybody turn and look. 'My F.F.M. is working! The climax of my life's work! Fact to fiction! Fiction to fact! The F.F.M. is working!'

And the F.F.M. began flickering and flashing and crackling on the end of the stall as if to echo his excitement.

The shoppers and the other stall-holders all looked at Wusster, then looked at each other, then laughed and returned to what they had been doing. Everyone thought that the old bookseller was completely mad.

But Robbie was grinning at Wusster like a Cheshire cat.

'I'll go and get the books from home,' he said as Wusster turned to face him again. 'I'm not going to school today.'

'So many holidays these boys have,' murmured Wusster, disapprovingly. He flicked a switch on the F.F.M., which whirred, wheezed, bleeped and fell silent.

Robbie dropped the skateboard on to its wheels and put one foot on it. 'Back soon!' he cried as he rattled away.

'One thing, Robbie!' Wusster called after him.

'Yes,' called Robbie from beyond the shellfish.

'Don't, under any circumstances,' yelled Wusster, 'be persuaded to go to Paperbackstack! Don't mix your *real* life with the story lives. You wouldn't want to end up stuck in a place that does not really exist, now would you?'

'Not blinking likely!' Robbie shouted from beyond the T-shirts. 'I wouldn't be so stupid!'

He reached the block of flats in record time

and, depositing his skateboard in the entrance hall, he sprang up the stairs. He burst in through the door of the flat, slamming it behind him and shouting, 'I'm here!'

7

The Packet

When he walked into the sitting-room, his mum was sitting in an armchair waiting for him, looking extremely cross. She had put her earrings on again and her coat was over a chair. 'Either you're ill or you're not, Robbie,' she said sternly. 'I've stayed off work so that you can be off school today and the least you can do before you dash off is tell me where you're going!'

'I'm sorry, Mum,' said Robbie shamefacedly. 'I don't feel too bad, now. Not like I did before. I don't think you ought to stay off work for me.'

'I *cannot* go to work, Robbie, if you are ill,' Mum stated flatly.

'I know,' said Robbie uncomfortably.

'Well, I'll tell you what we'll do,' said Mum after a moment. 'Since I'm not at work and since you're obviously not ill, we'll both go to see Grandpa and take him his books. The ones you bought from Wusster Dash. He'll be very pleased to get them.'

Suddenly Robbie froze, then he went dizzy, and then his head began to pound. He put his hand to his forehead and winced. 'I feel terrible again,' he murmured feebly. 'I think I need to go to bed. I'll take Grandpa his present tomorrow.' He staggered, reeling, to the living-room door. 'A short rest and I'll be fine,' he said, in the most reassuring voice he could muster. 'You go to Grandpa's, Mum.' He stumbled through the door and limped weakly, guiltily, to his room. He'd fooled Mum once that day. He knew he did not stand much chance of fooling her again.

'Robbie!' Mum called fiercely in a voice that made the ornaments rattle.

Obviously he hadn't . . .

'Robbie Wilson!' Mum yelled, hot with anger. 'What the dickens do you think you're playing at?'

But Robbie had already shut his bedroom door firmly and was leaning against it with his fingers crossed. He needed a miracle to get him out of this one.

The miracle came. The phone rang. Mum

stopped shouting and furiously picked it up.

'What do you want?' she snapped. 'Who is it?'

It was Mr Jade, her boss from the shop.

'Oh, Mr Jade, hello,' Mum said sweetly. 'How nice of you to call.'

Gasping with relief, Robbie darted across his room to look again at Grandpa's pile of books. He picked up *Gangsters 7*, opened it, took out the gangster's card and studied it.

Slim Jim's Gym and Health Club. The address was *14 Page Street, Paperbackstack 13*. On the other side of the card were the words *Compliments of the Boscoff Boys*, and pencilled into a space on the card were the words *3 Monsters, 7 Dreams, 9 Pops, That's All*. He did not understand it at all.

Robbie put the card back into his jeans pocket for the time being, and returned his attention to the books.

He could not possibly take them to Grandpa at the moment. Not with characters coming alive out of them all over the place. He must take them back to Wusster and exchange them for some others. There was no way that he could hope to make Mum understand that. The best he could hope for was that she would go to Grandpa's and agree to leave him on his own.

He'd wait a while and see what happened.

Listening very carefully, Robbie could hear that his mum was still on the phone. He swept the entire pile of paperbacks off the windowsill into his arms and sat down on his bedspread to look through them once again. He thought for a moment that the books were feeling warm and wondered how that could be possible, but then he decided that he must be imagining it. Underneath *Gangsters 7* was *The Oriental Gems*. The girl on the front cover looked frightened. That picture was still there, but seemed to be shimmering slightly and the jewels at her feet glowed.

Robbie was suddenly gripped by a chilling sensation. He looked around him, convinced, though he did not know why, that he was not alone. There was someone else in the room. Mum was still talking on the phone so he knew that it could not possibly be her. Robbie got up and walked uneasily across to the window and looked out. Nothing seemed unusual. He returned to his bed and picked up *The Oriental Gems* and, holding it in one hand, touched it thoughtfully with the other. No, he was not imagining it. The book was definitely warm!

At that moment there was a tiny cough from behind him, and he jumped. The cough sounded like water dripping on to a tin. Robbie swung around sharply. He looked, shut his eyes, then looked again.

There was a girl standing on his desk. She had black, shiny, shoulder-length hair, her skin was very pale, and her eyes were the shape of sugared almonds. She looked as though she could have come from some Far East country. She was holding a packet in her hands – a square brown envelope which seemed to have something hard inside. Her hand was trembling and her dark brown eyes were opened wide with fear.

'Take this for me . . . please,' she said, in a voice not much more than a whisper.

'Take what?' Robbie asked.

'This,' said the girl, thrusting the brown paper packet towards him.

'Why?' Robbie asked. 'What is it?'

'Don't ask,' she replied, 'but take it. I need a favour. Listen carefully to what I tell you. If I'm caught with it, I'm finished. . .'

'Finished?' echoed Robbie. 'What do you mean, finished?'

The girl put her hand to her mouth,

apparently too terrified to answer.

'Never mind,' he said. 'Go on. What is the favour you want?'

Tears squeezed out of the girl's eyes and slid down her cheeks. She bit her lip and continued with difficulty.

'The packet must be taken to my brother,' she said. 'The gangsters must not get it.'

'Gangsters?' Robbie interrupted. 'You mean the Boscoff gang?'

The girl hesitated and looked at him in some surprise. She twisted round and stood on tiptoe at the back of the desk, straining to peer out of the window.

'Is Mr Boscoff out there now?' Robbie said.

The girl turned back to him and her face was as white as paper. There was a loud roar then as a car pulled up outside. Car doors banged and men's voices could be heard.

The girl drew in her breath. 'Dear life!' she gasped. 'They're coming after me!'

Robbie did not like to see someone so small and frightened standing on his desk in such imminent danger of being 'finished', so he stepped forward.

'Give me the packet,' he said boldly.

The gangsters were only the size of monkeys.

Robbie was not afraid of them.

'I'll take the packet,' he said. 'I'll help you if I can.'

As the girl handed it to him, she looked up plaintively.

'Take it to my brother, Jim,' she whispered, 'at Slim Jim's Gym and Health Club. You know where Slim Jim's is?'

Robbie nodded. He knew where Slim Jim's was all right. He had the address there beside him. But Slim Jim's, Robbie knew, was in Paperbackstack. That was a fictional place and a place where he must not go. Wusster had told him that in no uncertain terms.

'Well, the trouble about me delivering a packet to Paperbackstack,' he began, 'is that I'm not allowed . . .'

But the girl who was, once again, looking out of the window, uttered a tiny scream and swung round with a look of horror on her face.

'Boscoff's coming!' she cried, 'I have to get away.'

She climbed elegantly out on to the windowsill.

'Don't hand that packet to anyone else,' she warned. 'No-one else but Jim.'

Robbie started as he heard the bustling sound

of his mother coming out of the living-room. The girl already had one leg out of the window. He looked towards the bedroom door for only a fraction of a second and when he looked back to the window, she was gone.

'Robbie!' Mum called gently from outside his door.

She had obviously calmed down quite a lot.

'Robbie! Are you all right now?'

'Fine,' said Robbie, gazing from window to door, bewildered.

'That was Mr Jade on the phone,' said Mum, opening the door, poking her head around and looking in with some suspicion. 'He says it's all right, me not going in today. Let's both go to Grandpa's now and take the books.'

'I can't come,' Robbie said. 'My throat's still sore. I still feel hot. I've got a cough.'

He made a sickly choking noise to demonstrate. He looked sheepishly at Mum and coughed again.

'Well, I'm going,' she said. 'I promised. Can I leave you on your own?'

'Yes,' insisted Robbie. 'I'll be all right, Mum, honest.'

Mum smiled a bit. Robbie was obviously making excuses. Why, she did not know. But she knew he was fond of Grandpa. Perhaps he had his reasons after all. She shook her head despairingly.

'I don't know what to make of you,' she said. Drawing her head back, she pulled Robbie's door shut behind her.

'Phew!' Robbie gasped.

'See you later then,' Mum said. Then, as she went out of the front door she called, 'Take care! I'll phone from Grandpa's.'

'Fine,' called Robbie. 'See you later.'

'Phew,' he said again when he heard the front door close with a bang.

8

The Oriental Gems

Robbie waited several seconds to make sure his mum was not going to come back for something she had forgotten, and then he rushed over to the window. The girl had gone.

He dropped the packet on to the top of his desk, and grabbed *The Oriental Gems* from where he had put it. It felt very warm, and as he had expected, the colouring had drained from the illustration on the front. The shape of the frightened girl was still there, but only as an outline. Another character, from another of Grandpa's books, had come to life. He *must* get these books back to Wusster immediately.

Robbie picked up a sports bag lying next to his bed and began to pile the books inside. As he tried to put the last one in, it slipped from his grasp. When he tried to retrieve it there was a flash like something blowing a fuse. He drew his hand away quickly, then carefully reached out again, gingerly picking it up between his thumb and forefinger. He dropped it like a hot potato into the bag and swiftly zipped it up.

Then he put on his anorak. As he was doing that he looked at the brown square packet lying on the desk. Robbie tore the corner open a tiny bit, just enough to look inside. He couldn't see too well, so he shook the packet gently over the top of his desk. Just like sweets falling out of a box, the contents spilled out everywhere. The envelope was jam-packed full of dazzling, glittering jewels! Tiny jewels like the oriental gems on the cover of the book. There were diamonds, rubies, sapphires and emeralds. They lay in profusion on the desk, sparkling gaily. They must have been worth a fortune!

But the jewels were hot and the books were hot and the packet was hot and Robbie sensed that time was short. He pushed the jewels back inside the packet and Sellotaped over the hole he had made. Then he slipped the packet into the pocket of his anorak. He put on his anorak over his jeans and sweater. Picking up the sports bag he walked quickly from his bedroom through to the living-room. He was nearly out of the door when the telephone rang.

At first Robbie thought he wouldn't answer the phone, but then he thought it might be Grandpa. He was sorry he had not been able to go and see him. It was his birthday, after all. He dropped the bag and went to answer the phone.

'Hello,' he said.

There was silence and a crackling on the line. Eventually a voice at the other end replied. 'What ho, old boy,' it said.

'Spiff?' said Robbie in amazement. 'Spiff, is that you?'

How could it be anybody else? Robbie had never met anybody else who spoke like that.

'Yes, old fellow,' Spiff replied cheerfully. 'Just telephoning you for the address of the gym and health club. I'm close on the track of the gangsters. I don't want to lose them now.'

'Fine,' Robbie said. 'I was going to phone you but I didn't get a chance. Something happened.'

'Forget it. Not got too much time to talk, old chap,' Spiff butted in. 'If you could just give me that address.'

Robbie took the gangster's card out of his pocket and read, 'Fourteen Page Street,

Paperbackstack Thirteen. But Spiff—'

'Yes, old boy. What is it?'

'I've just met somebody else who wants me to go to Slim Jim's gym,' said Robbie. 'I'm not allowed to go there. Can you help me, do you think?'

'You met somebody else?' said Spiff. 'Somebody else from Paperbackstack? Tell me all about it, Robbie.'

And Robbie did. He started from the beginning and went right on to the end. He told Spiff about buying the books for Grandpa, and then about Wusster Dash and the F.F.M. He told him once again about the gangsters' visit. He told him about the hardback book on Wusster's stall. He told him about the frightened girl and then he told him about the jewels.

Spiff listened in silence. 'Crikey, what a wheeze!' he said.

'A wheeze?' said Robbie, mystified.

'Yes,' said Spiff. 'You've got the gems. The Oriental Gems. They're famous in Paperbackstack. They're someone's family fortune. You must bring them back immediately.'

'But Wusster said I must not go to Paperbackstack,' Robbie told him, 'and anyway I don't know how to get there.'

'Well, old boy,' Spiff replied, 'I can tell you how to get to Paperbackstack if you want to come. It's jolly simple really. I can meet you there. And we can solve the riddle of the Oriental Gems together. But as for the decision about whether you should come or not, you must work that out with the man who made the machine. You must sort that out with Mr Wusster Dash.'

'How can I get to Paperbackstack then?' Robbie asked, thinking that maybe, if only he could try, he could at least ask Wusster . . .

'Listen carefully. I'll only say this once,' Spiff told him. 'The Paperbackstack underground seems to have become connected somehow with the Stack Green underground. So, if you go to the station on the other side of the market, you'll find a temporary link in the system. Get in the lift there. Press the special button, ten centimetres from the floor. Do you hear me – a green button ten centimetres from the floor?'

'Yes,' said Robbie, concentrating hard.

'Stay in the lift until it stops,' Spiff went on, 'then get out. You'll be in Paperbackstack Green underground station. It's deeper than

Stack Green. The Paperbackstack trains run below yours. I'll be by the lift, waiting for you . . . that is, if you want to come, of course.'

Robbie found he was breathing very quickly. Of course he wanted to go. But could he?

'All right,' he said after a full minute of biting his lip and furrowing his brow and making drum noises on his teeth. 'All right, if I can, I'll come. I'll ask Wusster. I'll try. I don't know, but I'll try to come.'

'Good fellow,' said Spiff and immediately the phone went dead.

Robbie replaced the receiver, picked up the bag of books and slung it over his shoulder. Then, grabbing his skateboard on the way out, he made for the market square as quickly as he could.

9

Stack Green Underground Station

Robbie skateboarded past the greengrocer and the T-shirts and even went quite close to the shellfish because he was in such a hurry. He hurtled up to Wusster's second-hand book stall, leapt from the skateboard, cleverly sliding it away underneath the stall as he did so, and dumped his sports bag down on the counter.

'They're here, the books!' he cried urgently. 'Another of the characters has come alive!'

'Let me see,' said Wusster, impatiently.

Robbie unzipped the bag and took first one book and then another out to show him how the characters had disappeared from their covers.

'Extraordinary,' said Wusster scratching his stubble with a sound like someone sandpapering. 'Totally Wusster Dashedly brilliant!'

Robbie began to hand the books to Wusster one by one for him to examine. As he did so, he noticed that the books had become burning hot. The white spaces on the book covers were glowing eerily, and the sports bag was full of a wispy, blue and green, funny-smelling smoke.

Wusster grunted.

'It's a good thing you brought these books back to me now, Robbie,' he said, his face becoming deadly serious.

'Why?' Robbie asked, alarmed.

Wusster put his nose close to a book and sniffed.

'Smell that,' he said, passing it to Robbie.

Robbie did. It smelt like burnt toast. As he handed it back to Wusster, tiny blue sparks spat out in all directions. Wusster dropped it on the floor, stamped out the sparks and then tossed it into the bag. Quickly, he pulled the zip across. He looked at Robbie gravely.

'I'm sorry to have to tell you,' he said, 'but soon these paperbacks are going to explode!'

'Explode?' echoed Robbie, absolutely horrified. 'Why?'

'The F.F.M. has indeed worked on these books,' Wusster explained. 'It has, indeed, temporarily turned the fiction into fact. But my experiments on the F.F.M. are very young. At this stage the transformation cannot last long.

These books were activated days ago. Their time is nearly over. What's happening now is the result of the fact-to-fiction process having run its course. These books must be deactivated right away. The fact and fiction experiment, for now at least, is over.'

'But it *can't* be over,' Robbie murmured, and he squeezed the envelope of jewels he had in his anorak pocket and wondered what would happen to them after deactivation.

'What's going to happen to the characters who have come alive,' he asked Wusster, 'if the books explode, or if you deactivate them?'

'Oh, sadly, if they are out of their books, they will be locked out of their proper place for ever,' said Wusster, shaking his head. 'But there's nothing else I can do.'

Robbie didn't answer. He looked at the clock that was clamped to the top of the F.F.M. It was ticking ominously. The hands stood at exactly 1.05 p.m.

'I was hoping,' Robbie began as he traced a number five with his finger on the top of the F.F.M. 'I was hoping, you see . . .' and his mouth felt so dry he could barely talk.

'Well?' said Wusster.

'I have something here to take to Paperbackstack,' he blurted out. 'Jewels. I promised a girl. Spiff is waiting to meet me.'

'Impossible! No!' Wusster broke in loudly. 'That would be most dangerous! After deactivation you would be locked in the fictional world for ever.'

Robbie produced the brown lumpy envelope from his pocket.

'Well, what shall I do with the packet of jewels?' he said. 'If I don't deliver these, a girl will be finished.'

Beads of sweat appeared on Wusster's forehead as he examined the packet and its contents. He had never intended to invent a machine that would endanger people's lives, but suddenly it seemed that that was exactly what he had done. Wusster used the scarf he was wearing around his neck to mop his brow. Then he put both hands on Robbie's shoulders.

'Look, my young friend,' he said, 'if I don't get the books into the machine in the next hour or so, there will be a major catastrophe!'

The bag was practically obscured now by a cloud of green smoke.

'Unless,' Wusster said, breathing in deeply, 'unless . . .'

Robbie feared that Wusster would never

breathe out again, but he did at last.

'Let's put it this way.' He scratched his beard noisily. 'Maybe,' he went on, 'maybe I *could* hold off the explosion for a while if I put the books in the fridge. On the fish stall, that is, to keep them cool.' Robbie shuddered at the thought. 'But it's a risk and I can hold off deactivation for no longer than an hour. Maybe, at a stretch, two hours.'

Robbie's eyes widened.

'You mean that you could give me an hour to go to Paperbackstack?' he asked.

Wusster shrugged.

'Maybe,' he said, 'maybe not. At least I can try.'

'Then I can go?' Robbie ventured.

The corners of Wusster's mouth turned up slightly. 'You'll be going somewhere that no person has ever been to before,' he said. 'You'll be alone.'

'No, I'll be with Spiff,' Robbie told him.

Wusster nodded.

'It will be the adventure of a lifetime,' he said, his face creasing up into a full-blown smile. 'And it will be available to you, all courtesy of Wusster Dash's extraordinarily brilliant F.F.M.!'

He gave a great burst of his donkey laugh. Everyone around the stall stopped to look at him. Robbie laughed as well.

'Go, Robbie,' Wusster said, and wagged his finger right in front of the boy's nose. 'But make sure you are back in an hour. If you were to get stuck in a fictional world, I should never forgive myself!'

Leaving his skateboard under the stall and the bag of books in Wusster's care, Robbie hurried off as quickly as he could to the underground station with the packet tucked well inside a pocket in his anorak.

10

Paperbackstack

At Stack Green underground station, Robbie stepped inside the big old-fashioned lift with several other people. They all stood like skittles, staring straight ahead. Robbie went down on his hands and knees and started searching around the walls. The green button was there but it was behind a woman's boots. The woman looked down at Robbie as he stretched to reach it.

'Whatever are you doing down there, darling?' she said. 'No offence, but I thought you were a dog.'

'Sorry,' said Robbie, 'I've dropped my conker.'

'But the lift floor's grubby!' said the woman. 'You'd better leave your conker. If it's there, you'd better leave it.'

Robbie put on his best disappointed look.

'It's really hard. A champion, kept from last year,' he insisted.

The woman shook her head. 'Kids!' she said, and gave the man standing next to her a look that said it all, but she stepped to one side and Robbie managed to press the little green, glowing button about ten centimetres above the ground.

He stood up and waited expectantly. Would something strange happen to him and all these other people in the lift, he wondered. The lady in the boots moved back in front of the flashing light. Robbie looked at her, smiled, looked away, looked at her boots, smiled at her again, then looked at the lift ceiling and drummed with his tongue on his teeth. Nothing strange happened. At least, not right away.

The lift stopped. Robbie stopped drumming. The doors slid open. The lift had reached the level of the overworld underground trains. The other passengers piled out. Robbie watched them go, but he stayed put. The green light was wobbling now and it soon began to wink. As the boots lady moved away, Robbie moved to stand in front of it.

'You're not getting out, darling?' enquired the booted lady as she left.

'Er, no,' said Robbie, reaching for another excuse and noting with some concern how brilliant he was becoming at thinking them up.

'Er, no, I've just remembered, I'm supposed to be taking my grandfather's dog to the vet.'

As he said that, the lift doors slid shut and he became separated from the ordinary under-ground, from the ordinary people of Stack Green. The lift stood still for a split second and then it began to descend. Robbie had the sense of covering a vast distance and the feeling that his insides were travelling further and deeper than the rest of him. He felt strangely scrunched and compacted, and things around him seemed to stretch like images in a distorting mirror. His surroundings became very large – very large and very odd. There was an uneven bump and then everything stopped.

The doors clunked open. Robbie stepped through them. He was in a station, much the same as Stack Green underground station, which must have been somewhere above him. This one was called Paperbackstack Green. Tunnels ran off, round and black, to Robbie's left and right. The heavy coaly smell was just the same as in a normal underground station.

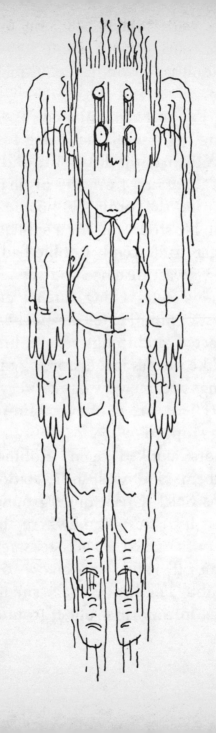

Everything was quiet except for the distant rumble of trains passing along other tunnels, and the station was deserted, except for a lone figure in a tweed suit with knee-length trousers, black socks and a pair of round-lensed, wire-rimmed spectacles balanced precariously on his nose. It was Spiff Carruthers.

Robbie tried to take the brown paper packet out of his pocket but it would not come. It seemed suddenly to have grown very large and had actually torn a hole in the lining of his anorak. He tugged the packet and eventually succeeded, by bending it over and tearing the pocket some more, in wrestling it out. Robbie held the packet in his hand. It had grown huge. He could feel the jewels inside it. Now they were as big as conkers!

Spiff stood still as Robbie approached slowly, cautiously at first, then faster, and then, with a hop, skip and a jump, he was by his side. Spiff and Robbie were the same size now. Like the packet of jewels, the boy detective had somehow quadrupled in size. The bigger Spiff had bigger teeth than ever. His spectacles were just as difficult to control. They slipped off as Spiff turned excitedly towards Robbie. 'What ho, old boy,' he said before he bent to pick them up.

'I've brought the jewels,' said Robbie, holding up the packet to show him.

Having replaced his spectacles, Spiff grabbed the packet, tore it open and poured some of the jewels out into his open hand. The Oriental Gems glittered magnificently.

'Cripes,' said Spiff. 'How absolutely splendiferous they are! I read about these jewels in the paper. They're famous. They were recently inherited by two young people, a brother and a sister living in Paperbackstack, who want to use them for the good of the community. But the Boscoff gang have been trying to get their hands on them. No deed is too wicked for those villainous scoundrels.'

'Well, the gangsters haven't got them now,' Robbie pointed out. 'I've got them and I'm going to take them to Slim Jim. I told the girl I would.'

Spiff looked at the jewels one last time, then returned them to the packet.

'We'll deliver them together, old boy,' he said. 'Just show me the gangsters' card.'

Robbie took the card out of his jeans pocket. It too was four times as big as it had been when he had last looked at it. Slowly the truth was dawning on him. It was not these things that had grown. It was he, Robbie, who had shrunk. The peculiar descent in the lift had shrunk him to the size of a monkey. His mouth went dry when he thought about the possibility of meeting up with full-sized gangster villains. But he was here now and if he met them he would have to be brave. He wished he could do karate.

Robbie showed Spiff the gangsters' calling card. Spiff looked at the address on it and nodded. 'I know where that is,' he said. Then he studied the scribbled words.

3 Monsters

7 Dreams

9 Pops

That's all

'And what do you suppose these words mean?' he said to Robbie. 'Do you think they are some sort of code?'

Robbie shrugged.

'I don't know,' he said. 'They don't make sense to me.'

Spiff read the words again.

'Nor to me,' he said thoughtfully. 'I'm

completely baffled. But you mark my words. Either I'm a monkey's uncle or this card will turn out to be a most important clue.'

Spiff put the gangsters' card in his pocket, sniffed energetically and rearranged his glasses on his nose.

'Follow me,' he said. 'We must make our way to Slim Jim's gym before the trail gets cold.'

He turned and set off up the slope of the buff-tiled passage, with Robbie following enthusiastically behind.

11

Slim Jim's Gym and Health Club

Robbie and Spiff hurried along the crowded pavements of Paperbackstack. They arrived, eventually at Slim Jim's Gym and Health Club. The main door was squashed between a video club and a hairdresser. It had a large notice suspended above it.

SLIM JIM'S GYM AND HEALTH CLUB

Belts of White and Yellow,
Orange and of Green.
Belts for Those Who Stick the Course,
Complete our Training Scheme.

Belts of Red and Purple,
Belts of Brown and Black.
Once the Black Belt's Round Your Waist,
You Won't Need to Come Back.

As Spiff and Robbie were reading the notice, the door flew open. A huge man was ejected through it. He flew like an enormous cherub across the pavement and landed heavily a metre or two away. His trilby hat soared like a bird behind him. The door was slammed shut noisily.

The ejected man lifted his head and shook his fist furiously. He was completely bald and had ears like broccoli. He lumbered to his feet, brushed himself down and growled. Then he replaced his trilby hat on top of his shiny head and loped off to a waiting car. As he stepped inside, with a great roar of the engine, the black limousine pulled away. Robbie and Spiff stood in a cloud of dust, gazing after it.

'I know that man,' Robbie said. 'I recognize him.'

'One of the gangsters?' Spiff suggested earnestly.

'Yes,' said Robbie. 'Fist's his name. He was in Stack Green this morning.'

'Was he indeed?' Spiff said, reflectively. 'Well let's see what he's been up to at Slim Jim's Gym and Health Club.'

He walked up to the door beneath the Slim Jim sign. There was a bell in the door. Spiff rang it twice. A crackly voice spoke as if from nowhere.

'What do you want?' it said.

Robbie and Spiff looked all around. They could see no-one except people passing in the street, but there was a small speaker fitted beside the door and the words *speak now* were illuminated.

'What do you want?' said the voice a second time.

Spiff leant towards the speaker. 'My chum has got something to give to Slim Jim,' he said.

'If it's got bullets and goes bang, buddy, you'd just better forget it,' said the voice, and the entryphone went dead.

Spiff rang the bell again. When *speak now* lit up, he nudged Robbie who said, 'I have a packet to give Slim Jim. It's very important.'

There was a moment's hesitation.

'You guys ain't gangsters?' the voice hissed suspiciously.

'No,' said Robbie and Spiff together. 'Gangsters? Us? Not likely! No!'

A buzzer sounded, Spiff pushed the door open and walked inside. Robbie followed. The door slammed shut automatically behind them. They found themselves standing in a magnificent gym, a wide, airy hall with exercise machines in every corner and climbing rails around the walls.

'Show yourself to the camera,' a voice commanded from a hidden speaker. 'Walk into the centre of the gym.'

Robbie and Spiff obeyed.

'Identify yourselves,' the voice went on.

Spiff stepped forward a little and looked towards a camera fixed high up on the climbing rail.

'Spiff Carruthers,' he announced. 'Intrepid boy detective from the hardback children's classic, *Spiff Solves Another Riddle.*'

'And the other guy?' said the voice.

Robbie stepped forward shyly.

'Robbie Wilson,' he said.

'What book?' said the voice.

'Er, *Stack Green Underground Station,*' said Robbie, knowing that, as titles of books go, this was not a very good one. Still, he had more important things on his mind. He pulled the packet out of his anorak pocket and held it up towards the camera.

'The packet,' he said. 'I've brought it all the way from Stack Green and I won't give it to anyone but Slim Jim.'

Nothing happened then for quite a long time. Robbie and Spiff stood waiting. They both jumped, startled, when a door flew open violently, as though it had been kicked from the other side. There was a fearsome howl, which sounded like an exuberant hyena. In through the door sprang a skinny, black-haired man – no shoes on his feet, white baggy trousers, white jacket secured by a long black belt, and black shiny hair in a fringe that hung over his eyes. He came to rest half a metre in front of Robbie and Spiff, crouched like a coiled spring and positioned ready, it seemed, to either attack or fend off attack – whichever turned out to be the most appropriate.

'Cripes!' exclaimed Spiff, 'a fighter!'

'A karate fighter!' Robbie gasped in admiration. 'A black belt karate champ.'

The man stared at each one of them hard, made some circular motions with his hands, shouted *'Yah yeeeh!'* at the top of his voice, then relaxed into a normal position.

'OK, you guys. Let's have a look at what you've brought me in this packet.'

'Are you Slim Jim?' Robbie asked.

The karate black belt nodded, thrusting his hand forward, palm up.

'The packet,' he said. 'Where did you get it? Who's it from?'

'Your sister,' Robbie said.

Jim's mouth dropped open. He pushed his fringe back and his almond-shaped eyes grew fierce.

'Jazzy?' he exclaimed. 'You've seen her? When? Where? Are you two more of the Boscoff mob?'

Spiff and Robbie stepped backwards.

'No, no. Calm down, old chap,' Spiff said.

'Here's the packet Jazzy gave me,' Robbie said, and he stepped towards Jim, smiling reassuringly. He did not want to be chucked out in the way that Fist had been earlier.

'Robbie, stop. Not yet.'

Spiff grabbed Robbie's arm and slapped his hand on top of the packet.

Jim's suspicions were aroused again and he leapt back immediately into the crouched karate position, hands raised and ready to attack.

'This *is* a trap!' he declared. 'I knew it from the start.'

Robbie wondered what Spiff was up to now.

'What are you doing, Spiff?' he gasped.

'Don't be alarmed, old boy,' Spiff said. 'I'd

just like to hear the answers to some questions first.'

Jim scowled at Spiff but after a moment he relaxed and straightened up.

'OK, OK. What do you want to know?' he said.

'Well,' Spiff said, running his fingers through his sandy curls and then taking off his glasses to polish them with a handkerchief. 'We ran into a dastardly wretch outside your gym. If you can tell us what his mission was, my chum here will be glad to hand over the packet. Robbie, is that right?'

Robbie shrugged and nodded. He didn't see any harm in that.

It took Jim a moment to decide, but eventually he let his hands drop to his sides in a gesture of despair. His black fringe fell over his eyes again, and his shoulders sagged as he pulled out a letter from the folds of his karate suit.

'That gangster guy, Fist, that miserable dirty rat, brought me this letter,' he said through gritted teeth. 'I threw him out, of course. . .'

Robbie quietly calculated that Fist was just about twice as big in every direction as Jim and very much more muscly.

'This is the letter,' Jim went on as he held up a large square sheet of paper. 'And when you read it you will see why things are looking bad.'

'Let's see it then,' said Spiff.

Jim handed the letter to Spiff, who read it, said, 'Cripes!' and passed it on to Robbie. He read it aloud.

We have your sister at our headquarters. If you want to see her again you must give us your family fortune, the Oriental Gems. We will accept no excuses. Await a further message.

The Boscoff Boys

'Those ratfinks have kidnapped Jazzy,' Jim told them grimly. 'The only hope I have of saving her is to hand over the famous Oriental Gems. That alone would be bad enough, but something even worse has happened. The truth is that the Oriental Gems are missing!'

'No, they're not. . .' Robbie began.

'Shut up, Robbie,' Spiff ordered. 'Please continue, Jim, old chap. Please complete your story.'

Jim seemed glad to spill out the whole tale

to the boys. It seemed that the gangsters had been coming to the gym and health club for quite some time now. Boscoff even used the gym as a meeting place sometimes. He didn't want anybody to know the address he really operated from, so he never told anyone the whereabouts of his secret headquarters. The gangster boss had been pestering Jim and Jazzy to hand over the gems ever since he had heard about them. He said he needed more funds to run his organization. Jim and Jazzy didn't like the gangsters or the things they did. It was bad enough having them around the gym and health club all the time. They had no intention of helping to support their racket too.

'Come with me,' Jim said to Spiff and Robbie. 'I've got something I'd like to show you.'

Robbie and Spiff followed Jim out of the gym and into an office behind. There was a safe standing in the corner of the office. It was standing wide open and was completely empty.

'When I came into the office first thing this morning, this is what I found,' he said. 'And I couldn't find Jazzy anywhere. Jazzy is missing and the jewels are missing. Since Fist paid me that little visit this afternoon,' Jim continued fiercely, 'I know Jazzy's a prisoner. I don't know where. As for the jewels. . .'

He didn't go on. He shrugged despondently and slumped down in a chair.

Robbie refused to be held back by Spiff any longer.

'Look inside this packet,' he said, thrusting it forward into Slim Jim's hand. 'Somehow Jazzy managed to get these away from the gangsters. She gave them to me – asked me to bring them here. . .'

'The mobsters must have pursued her and taken her prisoner after she gave them to Robbie,' Spiff said. 'Brave girl that Jazzy. She managed to save the jewels.'

Slim Jim hastily opened the packet. The gems fell from it higgledy-piggledy, glowing and glittering all over the office floor. Jim's eyes grew misty with emotion. 'Why, that's sensational,' he breathed quietly. 'You've got our family fortune.'

He jiggled the gems about together in his hand for a moment, then he sighed. 'But,' he added, looking up. 'if it's the jewels or Jazzy, I guess I'll have to settle for getting my sister back. It's a miserable shame to have to do a deal with those weasels but, since we don't know where she's being held, we don't stand much chance of rescuing her.'

'I'm not so sure,' said Spiff, who was scratching his head and obviously considering the matter hard. 'The Paperbackstack police have been on the track of the gangsters for quite some time – I read it in the papers. Everybody knows that the Boscoff Gang operate their racket from a secret headquarters, a hideout, a centre of operations, somewhere under the cover of an ordinary shop or office. But nobody knows what or where that is.'

Everyone fell silent.

Eventually it was Jim who spoke.

'I wonder if this might help,' he ventured. 'It's a scrap of paper that fell out of Fist's pocket when I threw him out of the gym earlier. It doesn't make sense, but it might provide another clue.'

He reached once again into the folds of his jacket and produced a torn scrap of paper. He showed it first to Spiff. Spiff read it and gave it to Robbie.

7 Dreams

14 Monsters

That's all

Spiff and Robbie looked at each other when they saw the words. They were almost identical to the words that had been scrawled in pencil on the gangsters' card. A list of some kind perhaps. A code maybe.

'Have you seen those words before?' Jim asked.

Spiff and Robbie nodded their heads.

'But we're baffled by them too,' said Robbie.

'And yet I'm sure they are significant,' said Spiff. 'I may not know what those words mean now, but one thing's for certain. I shall not rest until I do.'

12

The Iron Grille

When Robbie and Spiff reached the station, they made straight for the passage along which Robbie had walked with Spiff when he had first arrived.

'That's the way you must go in,' Spiff said. 'The lift will take you back to Stack Green. I can't come with you. I still have clues to uncover, riddles to solve, an adventure to complete. Only then can I return to Hardback, content in the knowledge that I have foiled another plot.'

Robbie wondered, uncomfortably, whether the deactivation of the paperback books in Wusster Dash's F.F.M. was going to make any difference to Spiff's involvement in the Paperbackstack troubles.

He smiled wanly. 'Will I see you again?' he asked. 'Will I be able to help you in another adventure?'

'I cannot say,' said Spiff. 'It's a rum business, this. All a bit of a wheeze, mixing fact and fiction, fiction and fact. Who knows? I simply cannot say.'

The tunnel that led to the lift seemed long and dark now that Robbie had to walk down it alone, and he felt a little scared. There was a clock over the main station entrance. It chimed twice. Robbie knew that the books would have to be deactivated very soon.

Spiff was holding out his hand. Robbie took it and shook it firmly. 'Goodbye, old chap,' said Spiff. 'Absolutely super working with you.'

Spiff strode confidently away. Robbie turned and walked boldly down the passage alone. It seemed very, very long. Eventually, he reached the recess where he remembered the lift had been. But then he got an awful shock.

An iron grille had been pulled across the entrance to the lift and padlocked shut. A notice hung on the grille. *Closed for Repairs*. Robbie's heart dropped down into his trainers.

It can't be closed, he thought. It's my only way back home.

But closed it was.

Robbie took two bars of the grille in his hands, gritted his teeth and, letting out a loud

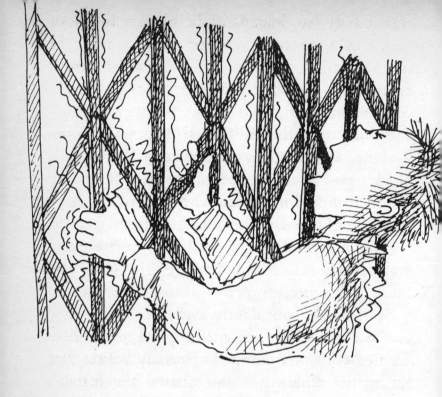

karate style *yay yee*, shook it with all his might. But it was useless. The grille just would not budge.

He had thought that there was no-one else about how he now realized that he was being watched. Behind him, a dark shadow stood humming in the gloom. Robbie spun around and saw a small plump figure. He blinked his eyes then looked again. The person behind him was a lady, a cleaning lady by the looks of things, a proper Mrs Mopp, with curlers in her hair, socks and slippers on her feet and a flowered overall tied tightly around her ample waist.

'What's the matter, ducks?' she said as she squeezed her mop into her bucket. 'You look like the end of the world has come.'

Robbie felt embarrassed because of the way he had just shouted. He looked confused and did not know what to say. 'Cat got your tongue?' the cleaning lady said.

Robbie shook his head.

'You don't want to go getting in a state about that silly old lift,' said Mrs Mopp kindly. 'Funny things have been happening inside that lift and no mistake. It's better that it's closed.'

That did not make Robbie feel any better at all and this must have showed on his face because the lady added, with a confidential nod, 'The workmen will be back to mend it later, I expect.'

'Later's too late,' Robbie told her gloomily. 'I need to get home right now or I might not get home at all.'

'The longest mile is the last mile home,' answered the lady, looking wise.

Robbie thought this was probably true, but he had not run out of ideas yet.

'Have you got a key to that padlock?' he ventured, hopefully. 'So I can use the lift. You can lock it up again as soon as I've gone.'

'Bless you dearie, no,' said the lady as she began to swish her mop about. 'But it's no use crying over spilt milk. There's many a slip 'twixt cup and lip.'

'Do you know who *has* got the key?' Robbie asked.

'The workmen took it, lovey,' the lady told him. 'They went to have their dinners. An army marches on its stomach. You know that, don't you dear?'

Robbie didn't really, but he nodded all the same.

'Where do the workmen have their dinner?' he asked her eagerly. 'Can I go and find them?'

The lady stopped washing the floor, squeezed out the mop, screwed up her mouth and had a good long think.

'Find them? Yes, I should think so,' she said eventually. 'They always go to McGreedy's Hamburger Bar. It's just around the corner. . . out of the passage, turn to your left. . . and up. . .'

Robbie didn't wait to hear the rest. Before another proverb could fall from the lady's lips he had sprinted off as if he had a pack of wolves behind him.

'More haste less speed!' the cleaning lady shouted after him. Robbie just heard this parting shot as he slipped over on the wet floor at the entrance to the passage and fell sprawling on to the pavement. Jumping to his feet again he hurried off. If only he could find the workmen. If only he could find McGreedy's Hamburger Bar, then everything would be all right.

13

McGreedy's Hamburger Bar

Robbie soon arrived, puffing and panting, outside McGreedy's. The workmen were somewhere inside. He did not know where but he intended to find out. People were coming and going through the red double swing doors. Robbie pressed his hands against the windows and squashed his face up close to look inside. It was hard to see clearly.

The windows were covered in mouth-watering pictures of the food which could be bought at McGreedy's. There were pictures of hamburgers oozing ketchup, ice-creams dripping chocolate, and bright gassy drinks, all spitting fizz.

Colonel McGreedy Welcomes You said a gaudy sign.

Try Our Monsters
Drink Our Pops
Eat Here

You'll Not Want To Stop
Chocolate Dreams
You'll Love Our Ices
Come Inside for Better Prices.

Robbie read the notice through and then he read it once again. *Monsters, Dreams, Pops. . .* Suddenly lights started flashing on and off in every section of his head!

Those scribbled words on Jazzy's scrap of paper! That scribbled list scrawled on the gangsters' card! Surely he thought, surely, those lists of things were orders to be taken away from here! *Monster* hamburgers, fizzy *Pop* drinks and chocolate *Dream* ice-creams! He slapped his hand to his head. It was all so obvious to him now. Why, he wondered, had it not occurred to him before?

Eagerly, excitedly, Robbie pushed open the double swing doors to take a look inside. He walked into the middle of the eating area and coolly surveyed the scene.

The lights were bright and there were dozens of people sitting on red plastic swivel chairs at yellow plastic tables. Many of them were eating hamburgers and chips. The walls were gaily decorated with painted flowers. On one side wall, looking out from a halo of petals, was the face of Colonel McGreedy. Robbie studied the face. He thought it looked familiar. Then it hit him. The smiling face of Colonel McGreedy was exactly the same as the face of the gangster boss who had appeared in his room that morning. Robbie realized, with a charge of excitement, which made him jump up into the air and clap his hands together, that Colonel McGreedy and Alberto Boscoff were one and the same person. He could hardly believe his luck. Could it be that he had accidentally discovered the Boscoff gang's front cover, their centre of operations, their secret headquarters, their hideout?

Robbie's only thought now was that he must get in touch with Spiff and tell him that the riddle of the gang's front cover was as good as solved. Jim must be told, the Paperbackstack police must be informed, Jazzy must be rescued and soon the troubles of this town would all be over.

Robbie turned to walk back across the bar and leave but, before he reached the door, a voice called out.

'Well hello, young Robbie.' Robbie stopped. The voice went on. 'May I call you Robbie? Would you like some hamburgers? Would you like some chips? How about a nice ice-cream? Come over here. I'm glad to see you decided to do business with us in the end.'

Robbie went as red as a cherry. He hadn't decided anything like that at all. He hadn't come to do business with the gangsters and he wasn't hungry either.

He turned around slowly. Behind the bar was someone else he had first met that morning. Someone with a tiny black moustache, a trilby hat, a striped McGreedy's apron and a very colourful tie. It was Smarto, the third gangster, the salesman. He was standing behind the hamburger grill, grinning broadly, waving and beckoning with a spatula.

Even worse, standing beside him was none other than the shiny-headed gangster strong man, Fist. Fist had a criss-cross plaster on his cheek and an impressive blue-black eye. That was thanks to Jim. He was tossing sizzling golden chips up into the air. They were fresh out of a large and foaming pan.

'Cripes,' thought Robbie, wondering where on earth he could have picked up an expression as strange as that. 'Some of the gangsters work in here and they've recognized me. That's blinking great, that is.'

Suddenly, Robbie's spirits sank. He felt like he had felt that morning, seeing Will Smith in the park. He wanted more than anything to turn and run, but he knew that he must not arouse the suspicions of the gangsters or they would escape before the police could come and arrest them. Smarto had called him over and he would have to go.

Struggling to fix a wooden smile on his face, he walked across the bar, looking as casual, cool and confident as he could. He stopped in front of the counter where Smarto and Fist were preparing food.

'So what can I make you, Robbie?' said Smarto. 'On the house, of course.'

'Er. . . nothing, thanks,' said Robbie. 'I've got to get home and see my grandpa. It's his eightieth birthday. He's expecting me. . .'

Smarto roared with laughter. 'Oh, very good,' he said, 'a very good excuse.'

'It's not an excuse,' Robbie protested. 'It's true.'

'Well, in that case, you'd better get on with talking business with the boss right now,' Smarto said. 'Come with me. You can wait in his office.'

If Robbie's heart had sunk into his trainers before, it was now several metres underground.

'All right,' he murmured. What else could he do?

Smarto put down his spatula and took off his apron. 'Watch the hamburgers, Fist,' he said to the big man standing beside him.

'All right, Smarto,' growled Fist obligingly and he picked up Smarto's spatula and used it to throw a hamburger expertly into the air. Seconds later, he caught it on a bun.

Robbie followed Smarto to a room at the back of the bar.

'Wait in there. I'll see where the boss wants to talk to you,' said Smarto, unlocking a door and opening it for Robbie to walk through.

Robbie walked into the gloomy, windowless office. The gangster pulled the door shut behind him and, with a loud and ominous rattle, twisted the key three times in the lock.

Robbie sat down on a leather chair which was standing beside a desk strewn with papers. He put his head in his hands. He was close to giving up. What chance did he stand now, he wondered miserably, of getting back to Stack Green in time? What would happen to him if he was stuck down here for ever? Fancy getting himself involved in a screwy business like this. How could he have been so stupid?

But, whether he had been stupid or not, there would be no point in blinking well giving up. Grandpa had often told him so. Wearily, he lifted his head from his hands, rose to his feet, summoned up a small amount of energy and began to look around the cluttered office.

And that was when he discovered, for the third time that day, that he was really not alone.

The silence of the office was broken by a squeal, followed by an angry grunt. Then there was the sound of a chair being rocked. Robbie peered into the darkness. Somebody or something was shuffling about fiercely in the far corner of the room. As Robbie moved closer he saw a frantic shadow swaying to and fro in a chair. The chair and the person tied to it fell over. Robbie darted across the room, turned on a desk lamp and looked down. Lying at his feet, her long hair awry, a gag on her mouth and an expression of sheer fury in her eyes, was Jazzy. She was four times bigger than when he had last seen her, but there was no mistaking her.

'Mm, mm, mm!' she said as loudly as she could under the circumstances.

Robbie bent down and tore her gag off.

'How dare you leave me tied up like this! Untie my hands and feet immediately!' she demanded as soon as her mouth was free. She looked up at Robbie scornfully, obviously mistaking him for one of the gangsters in the dim light.

'I didn't see you when I first came in,'

protested Robbie. 'I'm a prisoner in here too. . .'

'Well, untie me now,' cried Jazzy exasperated. 'I've got to get out of here. If Jim hands the gems over to Boscoff's mob, I shall never forgive him. . .'

Robbie found it hard to believe that this spirited girl was the same one who had cried in his room that morning. As he took the ropes from her wrists and ankles, she flexed the muscles in her arms and legs, muttering all the time about the way she would have dealt with the gangsters if she hadn't been outnumbered seven to one. When she was once again on her feet and had worked through one or two karate positions to get the blood flowing through her veins again, she turned to Robbie who was watching, perplexed. She studied him angrily for a moment, then her face broke into an enormous smile.

'Well, I'll be blowed. I didn't realize it was you,' she cried. 'You're the kid from Stack Green, aren't you? The big one. You're much smaller now. How'd you get so small and what are you doing here?'

Robbie dealt with the last of her questions first.

'You cried and asked me to bring a packet to

your brother,' he reminded her. 'I'm doing you a favour.' It occurred to him now with a shot of indignation that, if it hadn't been for her, he would never have got himself stuck down here in the first place.

'You got the gems back to Jim, kid?' she asked.

And just who does she think she's calling kid? Robbie thought with irritation.

'Yes,' he replied shortly. 'You seemed to be frightened this morning. You don't seem to be very frightened now.'

Jazzy giggled. 'Would you have taken the packet if I hadn't seemed frightened?' she asked.

'Probably not,' Robbie said.

'Well, there you are,' said Jazzy wickedly. 'I'm not frightened now. I'm angry. But thanks a million for the favour. I guess I owe you one.'

'What happened to you, anyway?' said Robbie. 'How did the gangsters catch you again?'

'They were on my trail all the time,' Jazzy replied. 'I only managed to dodge them for a few minutes, and hand the jewels over to you. They were lying in wait for me when I left your place and. . .'

She didn't have time to finish because

Smarto's voice could be heard outside the door. He was talking to somebody and obviously about to come in.

'We've got to get out of here,' Jazzy said, and Robbie agreed.

There was some quick thinking to be done. The wheels in Robbie's head were beginning to turn well now. As the adventure had progressed, he had found himself getting better and better at being a part of it. Somehow, now, he knew he was going to win.

There was a telephone on one of the office desks. It was half-hidden under some papers and the office lamp. Jazzy and Robbie both looked at it and both had a brilliant idea at the same time.

'We can phone for help,' said Jazzy.

'Yes,' Robbie answered decisively, 'and I know exactly who to phone.'

He still had Spiff's number in his pocket from that morning. He pulled the sheet of paper out of his jeans pocket and dialled as quickly as he could, hearing the phone ringing at the other end.

'Come on, come *on,*' he muttered, and drummed impatiently on the top of his mouth with his tongue.

Eventually, Spiff picked up the phone. 'Hello,' he said.

'Spiff, hello, it's Robbie. . .' Robbie said.

'What ho, old boy,' said Spiff.

'Spiff, listen carefully,' said Robbie.

Smarto was already turning the key in the lock. Robbie knew that time was desperately short.

'McGreedy's Hamburger Bar,' was all he said. 'Monsters, Pops, Dreams. . . The Boscoff Boys' headquarters.'

'Right ho, old boy,' said Spiff.

Robbie slammed down the phone just as Smarto entered the office. He swung around to face the gangster.

'Well, Robbie boy,' said Smarto as he bustled cheerfully in. 'May I call you Robbie?'

Robbie nodded.

'Mr Boscoff says he can see you now. Not in his office. He'll meet you in the bar.'

Robbie nodded again. All he needed now was time.

Jazzy had returned to the chair at the back of the room where she was sitting quietly in the shadows. Smarto didn't notice that her gag was gone and her ropes were on the floor. Robbie glanced briefly at her. Smarto saw the glance.

'I see you've found our hostage,' he commented.

'Yes,' said Robbie, giving away as little as he could.

'Proper little bag of energy, isn't she?' Smarto continued chattily. 'She's just a little insurance policy Mr Boscoff had to take out. Part of a business deal, you understand. . .'

'Yes,' said Robbie drily.

Biding his time, Robbie allowed the gangster to lead him out of the gloomy office and back into the well-lit bar. Smarto didn't think it necessary to lock the door behind him.

Robbie sat waiting at a table for what seemed like ages. Time was ticking on. Was there still time to get home? Of course there was. Robbie was a winner.

Eventually Colonel McGreedy, alias Alberto Boscoff, the boss of the Boscoff gang, made an impressive entrance from his office to the left of the bar. He walked towards Robbie, surrounded by an entourage of hoodlums. He made his way regally around the plastic tables and arrived eventually at the one where Robbie sat. Settling himself on a plastic swivel chair opposite, he waved his bejewelled hand. 'So, you've decided to join the Boscoff racket after all?' he said. 'Well, Robbie boy, welcome to the gang. You'll make an excellent villain. Nice to have you with us. . .'

14

The Police Raid

Robbie never really knew for sure exactly what happened next. He assumed that Spiff must have alerted the police, because at that moment some sort of raiding party burst into the fast-food bar and things hotted up.

All of a sudden, a Monster McGreedy cheese-burger was hurled across the bar and landed with a *splat* on the Boss's forehead. The cheese curled itself around his ears and the ketchup dripped down his face. A piece of pickle plopped straight on to the table in front of him.

Mr Boscoff did not speak, but his face went pale with fury.

One of the hoodlums said, 'Boss, it's the cops!' and everybody ran for cover.

Fist grabbed an entire tray of ready-made Monster Mcgreedys and ducked behind the counter. Smarto filled his pockets with several handfuls of hot chicken nuggets and hid under a table. Boscoff panicked and ran first this way and then that. He settled eventually for hiding behind the door of the ladies' cloakroom. The rest of the gangsters, and some of the customers, took up sheltered positions wherever they could find them and took with them heaps of edible ammunition. Some of the people who didn't want to be involved managed to get out into the street.

Robbie saw Jazzy emerge furtively through the now unlocked office door and hide herself under a table. He crouched down where he was, under the smiling petalled face of Colonel McGreedy on the wall and put both his hands over his head for protection.

The battle began. Scores of McGreedy's Dreams sailed through the air and showered melba sauce over the raiders. McGreedy relishes cascaded into the chip pan. Fizzy pop rained down from the ceiling. Hamburgers swooped through the air like birds of prey. Rolls whistled past ears and landed heavily in all four corners of the room. Cheese, pickle and ketchup dropped like bombs, transforming the appearance of everyone and forming a sticky, slippery carpet on the floor.

The uniformed raiders were not doing well. They had underestimated the number of gangsters and the strength of their resistance. The barrage of flying food continued to come hard and fast. Just as it seemed that they might run out of ammunition and give the gangsters a chance to escape, there was a whine of sirens in the distance, heralding the arrival of police reinforcements.

With a loud screeching of brakes which made everyone in the bar stop throwing things and put their hands over their ears, a further stream of police cars drew up outside the building. Car doors opened and policemen poured through like water out of a leaky barrel. They rushed into the hamburger bar through all its entrances and exits.

Chaos and confusion reigned. Ice-cream-covered gangsters were handcuffed to ketchuppy policemen, crying, 'You'll never make charges stick!'

'We know how to handle slippery customers like you,' the policemen answered.

'No-one locks up Mr Boscoff for long,' wailed Boscoff as he was dragged, protesting, from behind the door of the cloakroom.

Robbie climbed to his feet, wondering what the time was. A policeman approached him.

'Come along, sonny, it's off to the police station with you,' he said.

'No, no, Constable, that's my chum!' objected a cheerful voice from behind him.

'Your chum, sir?' said the policeman, turning round.

'Yes, Constable, he's got another station to go to – an underground station – and it's urgent. If you'd be so kind?' Spiff politely shifted the policeman to one side and took hold of Robbie's arm.

'Come on, old chap,' he said. 'We'd best get our skates on. Got to get you to that lift and home. There's no time for delay.'

Robbie didn't have time to check whether Jazzy was all right or to tell Spiff about the padlock in the grille. Spiff took off again at such speed that Robbie had to follow him or lose him. He bounded out of the bar and along the crowded pavement. Robbie hurried after him. They wove amongst the Paperbackstack shoppers, dodging, bumping and apologizing as they ran.

At last, they arrived at the underground station and hurtled down the gloomy passage. They stopped dead at the lift recess. The grille was still firmly in place, padlocked, immovable, shut.

Spiff looked at Robbie in consternation. 'You didn't tell me it was padlocked!' he exclaimed.

'You didn't give me a chance,' said Robbie.

There was a sound like drumming at the entrance to the passage. Robbie and Spiff listened and realized that it was the sound of pounding feet.

'Someone's coming,' Spiff observed.

The footsteps came closer and two people emerged out of the gloom, running lightly, athletically. One was talking twenty to the dozen.

'Good gracious, it's Slim Jim!' Spiff said when he saw them. 'Who's that girl talking to him?'

'It's Jazzy!' Robbie exclaimed, pleased to see that she had managed to escape the riot and meet up with her brother. As Jazzy ran alongside Jim she was recounting, in graphic detail, how she had given a policeman who wanted to take her to the police station a piece of her mind, and how she had very nearly punched a gangster on the nose.

Jim and Jazzy ran up to Spiff and Robbie and stopped. They stood for a moment, looking flushed and breathing heavily. 'We couldn't let you go without saying goodbye, kid,' Jazzy said to Robbie eventually. 'Without you, we would have certainly lost our family fortune.'

Robbie smiled modestly and looked at his trainers. Spiff patted him on the back.

'Yes, goodbye old buddy and thanks,' said Jim, pushing his fringe back out of his eyes, grabbing Robbie's hand and shaking it hard.

Robbie's feelings were mixed. 'Well, I don't know about "goodbye",' he said with some concern. 'The lift's padlocked shut. It's my only way home. I don't think I can leave.'

Jim looked at the grille. 'Oh, that's no problem,' he said lightly. He looked at Jazzy who was studying the padlock.

'No problem at all,' she agreed.

'You've got a key?' Robbie asked, a dim ray of hope beginning to dawn.

'Heck, no,' said Jim, 'But Jazz and I have each got a mean karate chop.'

And, with that, he stepped towards the iron grille. Jazzy placed herself beside him. They assumed an expression of deep concentration, then settled themselves into a karate position, knees bent, hands up and palms inward. Uttering two extra-loud hyena cries that echoed and re-echoed along the passage, they leapt a metre in the air. About halfway through their descent, they screeched *'hah yo yah yeeh'* and smashed the sides of their hands down on either side of the padlock with such force that it snapped immediately, clanked open and clattered to the ground.

'There you are, you see,' said Jim. 'No problem. Anything to help a friend.'

Jazzy was dusting off her hands and sniffing. 'Yes, kid,' she agreed. 'I guess that's the favour that makes us even.'

Jim seized the iron grille and heaved it back to unbar the lift door. A green button glowed beside the door.

'Press the button, now,' said Jazzy.

Robbie looked at Spiff.

'Press it, old boy,' said Spiff. 'This really is a wheeze.'

Robbie pressed the button. Immediately the lift doors hummed apart.

'See ya, kid,' said Jazzy.

''Bye, old buddy,' said Jim.

'Cheerio, old chap,' said Spiff.

Robbie stepped inside the lift. Once he had done that, the doors clunked shut, dampening all outside sound. A faint whirring began and grew louder. A host of weird sensations over-whelmed him. An expanding feeling seeped through his arms and legs, his body and his head. It was like being a balloon with somebody blowing into it. The feeling stopped as suddenly as the lift did, approximately thirty seconds later.

The lift doors opened. Robbie had reached the level of the Stack Green underground trains. He could hear them rumbling in the tunnels beyond. A number of people, similar in size to Robbie but looking very much like the usual people at home, entered the lift and stood around him. The doors closed again. The lift continued going up. When Robbie stepped out at last he was at overground level in the well-lit and familiar Stack Green station. He raced gratefully outside and took in a huge and wholesome breath – a great lungful of overground air. He was very glad to be back in familiar territory and more than a little surprised to be safe!

15

Wusster's Fact/Fiction Machine

Wusster had already retrieved the fizzling bag of F.F.M.-activated books from the fish stall. Robbie had been gone not for one hour but for almost two, and Wusster was only too horribly aware of how essential it had become to deactivate the books without further delay. He didn't want to trap Robbie in Paperbackstack forever, but there was now nothing else he could do. He wiped a tear of sadness from his cheek with his scarf. He had been fond of the boy and was going to miss him.

Just then, Robbie arrived at the market square, breathless after his run from the station and bursting to tell Wusster everything.

'I'm here. I'm back!' he announced from behind the stall-holder, who was securing the doors of the van.

Wusster swung round. 'Robbie!' he cried

and threw his arms open wide, clamping them around the boy in a suffocating bear hug. 'The packet's delivered?' he asked. 'You're safe?' Robbie could only splutter because he was being held so tightly. Wusster released him and Robbie drew back and began to breathe again.

'Yes, I'm safe,' he said, grinning.

The bookseller looked at him and laughed like a donkey, his gold teeth glinting in the sunlight.

'Everything's all right. The police arrested the gangsters in the end,' Robbie said, 'and I helped save Jasmine and the jewels.'

'Wait a minute,' Wusster interrupted, raising his hands high into the air like a man conducting an orchestra. 'All that can wait. Now it is essential we get the books through the F.F.M. as soon as possible. They are already out of the fridge and *very* volatile.'

Even as he spoke there was a muffled explosion in the back of the van.

Wusster and Robbie spun round. The doors of the van had blown open and a thick cloud of smoke was billowing towards them. A single charred page of a book fluttered through the smoke and disintegrated at their feet.

'There goes one page,' muttered Wusster anxiously, 'and the rest may soon follow. Unless we want to lose all the books and blow up the market, I'm going to have to try and operate the deactivation right here!'

'Here?' said Robbie.

'Right here,' said Wusster, 'in the van. The stall has a mini-generator. I'll connect the F.F.M. to that. I think it'll work.'

'I'll help,' Robbie said, excitedly.

Wusster hurriedly ran a lead from the generator into the back of the van. As the smoke cleared, he and Robbie climbed inside, slamming the doors shut behind them. Although they were now crouching in complete darkness, Wusster had a torch which he turned on and it didn't take him long to fix up some more dim lighting. The F.F.M. was soon hitched up to the power cable and its many coloured lights began flashing on and off. The buzzing and clicking inside it began again.

On Wusster's instructions, Robbie looked inside the sports bag. The zip had been blown apart by the earlier explosion. Words and phrases had broken free of their pages and were shooting around in there like hot popcorn.

The first paperback Robbie took out of

the bag was *Gangsters* 7. Wusster took it from him and slipped it into the machine. All the F.F.M. lights stopped flashing immediately. A tiny screw fell out of a hole in the side. There was a dull glugging sound, like bubbles in sludge, and the machine regurgitated the book straight out on to the floor. After a second or two of heaving around, the book popped open and a further storm of words and pictures were released into the air.

'Is that what the machine's supposed to do?' Robbie said, perplexed.

'No,' said Wusster with a glint in his eye. 'This F.F.M.'s a bit like Wusster Dash. It seems to have a screw loose.'

He retrieved the screw and replaced it. Robbie picked up *Gangsters 7* from where it was lying on the floor. He handed it to Wusster, who inserted it into the F.F.M. Robbie gathered up the heaps of words, full stops, commas and quotation marks that had been thrown out and added them like currants in a cake mix.

'All systems go,' muttered Wusster as he pulled a lever. Lights began to wink on and off, slowly at first, then in a frenzied way. The buzzing and ticking began again quietly then worked up to a crescendo. There was a whine like a police car siren. The machine rattled, twirled, jumped up and down, clicked, buzzed and winked. Finally, the process was complete. *Gangsters 7* slipped silently out on to the floor.

Wusster picked it up. It was in a pretty dreadful state, bent, burnt and battered, but the picture was back on the front almost exactly the same as it had been before. Some of the gangsters had a few extra bumps and bruises and there were some spatters of pickle and ketchup on their clothes, but that did not seem too serious.

Soon *The Oriental Gems*, *The Karate Champ*, *Spiff Solves Another Riddle* and all the other books had been deactivated thoroughly. All the characters were back where they belonged. Everything was as it should be in Paperback-stack and Hardback and Stack Green. All was well.

Robbie and Wusster relaxed against the sides of the van. Wusster mopped his brow with his scarf, and Robbie grinned.

'We made it, then?' said Robbie after a long and exhausted silence.

'Yes,' said Wusster. 'Thank goodness for that. I really believe we did.'

16

Tea and Cake

Wusster opened the doors of the van and he and Robbie tumbled out into the marketplace.

'What would you say if I were to offer to treat you to a nice big hamburger and chips at McReady's when I close the stall?' Wusster said. 'I think it's fair to say you've earned it.'

Robbie thought that was a brilliant idea.

'Yes, that's great,' he said, 'but I'll have to go home and check with Mum. She may be back from Grandpa's now.'

Wusster turned round to reach back into the van and pull out Robbie's sports bag. It was scorched inside and the zip was broken, but it was the only one Robbie owned so he thought he had better take it home all the same. Some of the deactivated books were heaped up on the van floor, beside it. Robbie leant into the van and grabbed some of the paperbacks he had bought a few days before. He had been intending to put them into the bag to take home as well, but he realized now, with some concern, that they were in a terrible mess. They had been tattered before, but now they were singed, crumpled and blackened, with the pages curled and burnt. They were no longer fit to be a present for Grandpa's birthday.

'Grandpa was looking forward to getting these books,' said Robbie. 'I don't know what he's going to say when he sees them.'

Wusster reached into the back of the van and pulled out the one book that had gone through deactivation and was still as good as when it started. It was *Spiff Solves Another Riddle*.

'Take this instead,' he suggested. 'It's the sort of book your grandpa would have liked when he was young.'

It was better than nothing, Robbie decided.

'Thank you,' he said as he took the book from Wusster. He pushed it inside his sports bag, then, slinging the bag over his shoulder, he ran across to the book stall and pulled his skateboard out from underneath.

'See you later!' he cried as he climbed aboard and rattled off. 'And thanks!'

'Yes, Robbie, see you later.' Wusster said.

Robbie wove back amongst the stalls and people. It was getting on for a quarter to four and the end of the school day. Since he had stayed off school, Robbie didn't particularly want to be seen out and about. The other kids would ask him where he had been and it would be embarrassing. He put his head down and thundered past McReady's, in case anyone he knew was in there. He was just in sight of his own block of flats and feeling relieved, when he

noticed Will Smith sauntering along the pavement towards him. His first thought was to turn and skateboard in the other direction, as fast as he could. But he didn't. After all that he had been through that day, he decided that he wasn't in the mood to run.

'Hey, Scaredy, Scraggs, Stupid!' sneered Will, as he approached.

Robbie jumped off his skateboard, stamped on the back and flicked it up into his hand. He caught it first time. Blinking brilliant, he thought.

'Who do you think you're calling stupid?' he said to Will. 'I'm not half as stupid as you!'

If Will Smith was surprised to hear Robbie answer back like that, Robbie was ten times more surprised himself.

'Oh, we are getting cocky, aren't we?' said Will, a little less confidently. 'When are you coming back to school then, Shrimp? You don't look very ill to me.'

'I'll be back tomorrow,' Robbie said, 'but I'm not taking part in any karate match. You can forget that. I never wanted to. I'll take part in some sort of skateboard competition maybe, if you like. I'm better at that. But I'll have to see how I feel.'

One thing Robbie had learnt that day was that you don't get anywhere if you use all your imagination and energy making up excuses. It was better to face up to telling people the truth.

Will was totally flabbergasted. Robbie had always appeared to be scared of him, so he had always bullied him. Now Robbie had answered back, he simply didn't know what to say.

'Well, see you tomorrow then, Rob,' he muttered.

'Yes,' said Robbie, just as flabbergasted as Will. 'See you tomorrow.'

If he could handle Paperbackstack gangsters, he could handle Will Smith. Nothing to it, really.

Pushing his skateboard under the stairs, Robbie raced up to his front door and let himself in.

'I'm here!' he cried.

He burst into the living-room.

'I'm here,' he said again.

'So we notice,' Mum said coolly.

She was pouring a cup of tea for Grandpa, who was sitting spread out in an easy chair with his foot up on a stool and a piece of cake in his hand. He had a half-amused look on his face.

'Hello, Robbie,' he said. 'I expect you're surprised to see me here, but I got tired of waiting at home for you to bring me my present. I had to come here up all those blinking stairs to get it myself.'

'Oh, yes, Grandpa, sorry,' Robbie said. He wasn't too worried. He knew Grandpa liked to come round to the flat really, even though he always complained about the stairs. He sat down on the arm of the old man's chair and put his hand on his tweedy shoulder.

'Your mum's been promising me the books were on their way,' Grandpa continued, patting Robbie's hand, 'but I waited and they didn't come. So here I am.'

'Yes, Robbie, where are the books?' asked Mum. 'We've been looking for them everywhere.'

'Yes,' cried Grandpa, loudly. 'Where *are* the blinking books?'

'I had to take them back to Wusster,' Robbie explained. 'That's where I've been. They got into a terrible mess.'

He slipped off the arm of Grandpa's chair and picked up his sports bag. Unzipping it, he took out the old, green, hardback book.

'Wusster gave me this one instead,' he said,

handing it to Grandpa. 'He said he thought you'd like it.'

Grandpa took it without a word. He put the last of the piece of cake in his mouth, brushed some crumbs off his front, fumbled a pair of glasses out of a pocket in his cardigan, put them on and studied the cover of the book. It had a picture of a sandy-haired boy in a tweed suit with trousers down to the knees and black woollen socks.

Grandpa looked first at Mum and then at Robbie. 'Spiff Carruthers!' he exclaimed.

Robbie nodded.

Silently, Grandpa opened the book and flicked through the pages. Inside, the book seemed to be mostly words but there were some pictures as well. A huge, delighted smile was slowly spreading across the old man's face. He snapped the book shut, took off his glasses and looked at Robbie in quiet astonishment.

'Fancy you finding me a book about the intrepid boy detective,' he said, beaming. 'Spiff was always my favourite when I was young. Many's the time, in my own imagination, I've helped sort out a crime with Spiff Carruthers.'

Mum was so pleased to see Grandpa happy that she forgave Robbie almost completely for pretending to be ill, making up those stupid excuses and forcing her to stay home from work that day. She sighed, put a slice of cake on a plate and handed it to Robbie, then she picked up the teapot and looked at him kindly, warmly.

'Cup of tea now, love?' she said.

'Of course, it's different with boys nowadays.' Grandpa went on as if he had not been interrupted. 'Just take you, for example, Robbie. I can't imagine that a modern boy like you would want to have an adventure with a character from a book, not nowadays. No, things are very different now.'

Robbie shrugged, looked mysterious and took a bite of cake.

'Oh, I'm not so blinking sure,' he said. 'I don't know so much. Some boys might. . . Yes please, Mum. I'd like a cup of tea.'

THE END